"Do you lie to your mama with that mouth?"

"Fine." Eve huffed. "So I didn't go with the others and watched all of that go down with your parents and brother. I waited until you left the ballroom and went after you."

"Why?" Kenan rasped.

He felt rather than witnessed her shrug. The same with the small kiss she pressed to the middle of his shoulder blades. He locked his muscles, forcing his head not to fall back. Ordering his throat to imprison the moan scrabbling up from his chest. Commanding his dick to stand down.

"Because you needed me," she said.

So simple. So goddamn true.

He did need her. Her friendship. Her body.

Her heart.

* * *

The Perfect Fake Date by Naima Simone
is part of the Billionaires of Boston series.

Dear Reader,

I'm so excited that *The Perfect Fake Date* is finally here! Friends to lovers is one of my favorite tropes. And then throw in unrequited love? Sigh. I'm a goner. Just step right on over me, 'cause I'm going to relax here after this swoon. LOL!

There's something so sweet about friends who have a close, trusting bond suddenly seeing each other through different eyes. It's also scary. Because they have to face the risk of losing that relationship by reaching for something more. Something passionate. Breathless. And incredibly romantic and abiding.

In *The Perfect Fake Date*, Kenan Rhodes has been secretly in love with his best friend, Eve Burke, since they were teens. Plot twist, though—she's in love with his brother. Accepting she won't ever see him as anything other than her friend, Kenan offers to help Eve win her heart's desire if she assists him with his. Thus begins an entangled affair that neither sees coming. And the stakes are high...and hot.

I am so looking forward to you reading Kenan and Eve's love story, and I hope you love them as much as I do!

Happy reading!

Naima

NAIMA SIMONE

THE PERFECT FAKE DATE

Recycling programs
for this product may
not exist in your area.

ISBN-13: 978-1-335-73536-2

The Perfect Fake Date

Copyright © 2021 by Naima Simone

This edition published by arrangement with Harlequin Books S.A.

For questions and comments about the quality of this book,
please contact us at CustomerService@Harlequin.com.

Harlequin Enterprises ULC
22 Adelaide St. West, 41st Floor
Toronto, Ontario M5H 4E3, Canada
www.Harlequin.com

Printed in U.S.A.

USA TODAY bestselling author **Naima Simone**'s love of romance was first stirred by Harlequin books pilfered from her grandmother. Now she spends her days writing sizzling romances with a touch of humor and snark.

She is wife to her own real-life superhero and mother to two awesome kids. They live in perfect domestically challenged bliss in the southern United States.

Books by Naima Simone

Harlequin Desire

Billionaires of Boston

Vows in Name Only
Secrets of a One Night Stand
The Perfect Fake Date

Blackout Billionaires

The Billionaire's Bargain
Black Tie Billionaire
Blame It on the Billionaire

HQN Books

The Road to Rose Bend
Slow Dance at Rose Bend

Visit the Author Profile page at Harlequin.com, or www.naimasimone.com, for more titles.

You can also find Naima Simone on Facebook, along with other Harlequin Desire authors, at Facebook.com/harlequindesireauthors!

To Gary. 143.

One

"If you think I don't know that my purpose here tonight is being your beard, then you've seriously underestimated my role as your best friend. And my intelligence."

Kenan Rhodes glanced down at Eve Burke, the petite woman on his arm and the woman who'd just called him on his shit. And with a smile. She was classy like that.

He snickered, nodding to a black-suited server as he nabbed two flutes of champagne from the man's tray. After passing one to his best friend, he sipped from the other.

"You have such a suspicious mind. I think it's a by-product of being a high-school teacher. So used to having kids lying to you about homework and bath-room passes."

He smiled at yet *another* person staring at him, his mouth pulling tight at the corners. The older woman, draped in more diamonds than Cartier, dipped her head in acknowledgment before turning to the man next to her and whispering behind her gloved hand. Irrita-tion prickled under his skin, and he deliberately turned away from the couple.

"What's wrong?" Eve demanded, studying him through narrowed, dark brown eyes.

"Nothing."

She arched an eyebrow. "You're rubbing your thumb over the scar on your jaw. Do I really need to point out you only do that when you're contemplating world domination or when something—or someone—is both-ering you?"

He dropped the hand he hadn't even realized he'd lifted to his face down to his side and shot her a dis-gusted look. Sometimes he *really* hated having some-one in his life who knew him so damn well.

"Fine." He paused, annoyance and frustration crawl-ing through him again. "It's been six months. Six. Months. Eve. And still they're staring like I'm a side-show act in a circus. Like we all are. As if we're all in their midst for their entertainment."

Admittedly, his entire world had been flipped on its ass when he'd received a certified letter request-ing his presence at the reading of Baron Farrell's will. Baron Farrell. The longtime CEO of the international, multibillion-dollar conglomerate Farrell International with the reputation of being a brilliant businessman and a ruthless bastard. Why he'd wanted Kenan, a marketing vice president in his family's successful commercial-real-estate development company, to attend his will reading had been a mystery. A mystery that had been quickly resolved when Kenan discovered he was Baron's illegitimate son. According to the will, Kenan and the two half brothers he'd had no idea existed had to stay together and run Farrell International together for a year or else the company would be broken into pieces and sold to the highest bidders.

Brothers.

Cain Farrell, the acknowledged heir Baron had kept and raised. And Achilles Farrell, a computer software designer and tech genius from Tacoma, Washington, whom Baron had abandoned, just as he'd done with Kenan. But Achilles had been raised by his single mother while Kenan had been adopted by his parents and raised in Boston.

Oh, yes. For the last few months, since the story had broken, Boston society had had a field day about the Farrell Bastards, as they'd dubbed Achilles and Kenan.

Eve's hand wrapped around Kenan's and squeezed, drawing him from his morose thoughts.

"They're small people with small lives who breathe for any hint of scandal or gossip to brighten up their existence. And let's face it, *the* Baron Farrell of Farrell International fathering two unknown sons? Sons he grants co-ownership of his company on his death? That's the kind of drama these people *live* for. But just because they're staring at you like a sideshow act doesn't mean you have to perform. You're Kenan fucking Rhodes. You don't dance for anyone."

Clearing his throat, he lifted his glass. "Drink your champagne," he murmured.

Smirking, she did as he ordered. But then responded, "You're welcome."

He glanced away from that quirk of her wide, sensual mouth on the pretense of scanning the crowded ballroom. Either that or risk letting Eve glimpse the secret he'd managed to keep hidden for fifteen of his thirty years.

It wouldn't do to reveal in front of God, country and all the guests attending the annual Brahmin Arts Foundation gala that he was in love with his best friend.

Unrequited love.

His hold tightened on the glass, matching the constriction squeezing his chest. Such a fancy, completely inadequate way to describe the hell of having your heart broken day after day when the person you crave more than air looks at you with wholesome…affection.

It killed a part of him.

And every time she brushed those soft, almost too-full lips over his cheek in a platonic kiss, or pressed her sexy, lush curves against his body in an amicable hug, another piece of him died another death.

"So tell me—" Eve nudged him with her elbow "—what overzealous socialite am I warding off tonight?"

He inhaled, taking in her earthy musk of cedarwood, roses and the shea butter she'd massaged into her skin for as long as he'd known her. If he was blindfolded and shoved into a warehouse filled with thousands of open perfume bottles, he would still be able to select her erotic, hedonistic scent. It teased him when he was awake and haunted him in his sleep. He couldn't escape it—couldn't escape her.

Even when he prayed to. And, God, sometimes he did pray that he could exorcise this damn love for her from his heart, his soul.

Sweeping his gaze over the packed ballroom of the former turn-of-the-century hotel, which was now an art museum, he quickly located a woman who would provide a suitable scapegoat to satisfy Eve's curiosity. Fortunately—or unfortunately, depending on the point of view—the woman seemed to sense his scrutiny and smiled in his direction, the invitation in her gleaming eyes clear and unmistakable.

"Never mind." Eve snorted. "Question answered. And I should've known. She's just your type, too."

"My type?" Even knowing he'd probably regret asking, Kenan did, anyway. Because one of the prerequisites of being in love with an unavailable, oblivious woman? A healthy dose of masochism. "What does that mean?"

She shot him a look that might as well have had the caption "Seriously? Is this what we're doing?" underneath it.

"Almost as tall as you. Size two, or hey, I'll be generous, a three. I'm betting on hazel or green eyes. And I'm not accusing you of colorism, mind you, but I *am* saying she's passing the 'brown paper bag' test. Also, her hair is ruler-straight either by a great keratin treatment or with the best Brazilian weave money can buy. And she's flawless. Like, 'a blemish would be too humiliated to do something as plebian as mar her face' flawless." She arched an eyebrow. "Ring a bell?"

Yes. In other words, the women he dated—he fucked—were anti-Eves.

Tall where Eve was petite. Slender where she was curvy and thick. Light, multihued eyes instead of a chocolate, nearly black shade that he could fall into. Fairer-skinned instead of a smooth mahogany that he hungered to drag his fingers over. Straight hair instead of the explosion of beautiful, dark brown natural curls that framed Eve's fascinating assembly of delicate bone structure and large, bold eyes, nose and mouth.

There was one area she wasn't their opposite—one area those other women couldn't compete at all.

Flawless?

Eve Burke was incomparable.

He bowed his head over hers, adopting a smirk. Pretended he wasn't affected by this fragile dance of innocuous flirtation and friendship. He was a pro, after all.

"I didn't know you paid such close attention to who I…entertained," he teased. "I have a question, though. Why do you care?"

She shrugged. "I don't. But it doesn't bother you to be so…cliché?"

Her criticism was a bee sting he couldn't dig out from under his skin. Because it was her. Because she had no fucking clue.

An unreasonable anger stirred within him, goading him to push, to sting back.

"Bother me?" He leaned farther down until their foreheads nearly brushed, until he could almost taste her champagne-flavored breath. Could feel the hitch of her swift intake of air on his lips. "Why should it? I'm not marrying them, Eve. Surely, you've heard the rumors about me. I know I'm your friend and you might consider yourself to be on the periphery of Boston society, but you're not deaf. You're smart. You read gossip columns." He dropped his voice to a murmur, narrowed his eyes on her mouth and studied the plump, overripe curves, before lifting his gaze to her eyes. "You know what those women use me for just as much as I enjoy being used."

Silence and a tension that damn near hummed sprung up between them. She didn't move, and neither did he. In a sea of people, they were statues, the tides of the crowd flowing around them as they stared at each other.

His words echoed in his head, over and over, the taunting tone growing louder, and an ugly part of him—the part of him that resented her for not *seeing* him, not *wanting* him—rejoiced at the shock that parted her lips, darkened her eyes.

But, God… His cock thickened, hardened behind his tuxedo-pants zipper. Lust and wonder, one a demanding howl, the other an awed whisper, twisted and purred inside him. Clawed and petted. Left him struggling not to reach out and stroke the tender skin beneath those beautiful eyes.

Eyes where desire glinted.

For…him.

Fuck.

Yearning pumped through his veins, piping hot like the strongest coffee, and it shot through him with the same kick of adrenaline.

"Eve…" he murmured.

"Kenan. Eve. I thought I saw you two."

Kenan stiffened at the intrusion of the new but familiar voice that doused him in a frigid wave of reality. Slowly, he stepped back from Eve and turned to face his older brother. Forcing a smile to his face, he pulled Gavin Rhodes into a hug, clapping a hand to his shoulder. He didn't glance back as Gavin greeted Eve—couldn't.

Not when he grappled with the truth and couldn't risk allowing either of them to glimpse the pain tearing into his chest before he managed to conceal it.

Because with Gavin's appearance, he got it.

That desire in Eve's eyes hadn't been for him.

God, how could he be so stupid, so foolish, to forget?

The only thing worse than being secretly in love with his best friend was for his best friend to be in love with another man—his brother.

"Eve, you look beautiful," Gavin said.

"Thank you, Gavin."

Kenan didn't have to peek down at her to catch sight of the pretty blush that undoubtedly painted her graceful cheekbones, or how the fringe of her lashes would sweep down and hide the adoration in her eyes. He'd witnessed her reactions to his brother's presence so many times they were branded in his brain like scar tissue.

He also didn't need to look at his brother to know Gavin would take in the thick curls brushing skin bared by her off-the-shoulder, deep red, mermaid-style dress and only see their father's executive assistant's daughter, and not a sensual, gorgeous woman who stared at him with need in her eyes.

Gavin might be heir apparent to the Rhodes family business—groomed to be even before they'd adopted Kenan—but he was still a "blind as fuck" idiot.

Bitterness, hot and caustic, crawled through Kenan. And he hated himself for it. Especially since he should be used to it by now.

Coming in second in a father's love was an old, sad story. Spare to the heir? So unoriginal.

Yet, it was the reason he couldn't bring himself to reveal the truth about his feelings to Eve. He might be second best in love and in business to his father. But he couldn't bear to be second best with her.

Not with Eve.

"Where are Mom and Dad?" Kenan asked.

"Dad was held up by Darren and Shawn Young. They wanted to talk about a possible new project in Suffolk Downs." Gavin cocked his head to the side. "Just a heads-up. Darren mentioned your name and what it would mean to have you involved. I think Dad intends—" He broke off the rest of the sentence, nodding and smiling over Kenan's shoulder. "Be right back. Duty calls," he grumbled, still wearing what

Kenan labeled the "social smile." Gavin clapped Kenan on the shoulder and strode away.

Leaving Kenan with a hollow pit in his gut.

"I heard what he said." Eve stared after him. Hell, did she even realize that she couldn't hide the hunger, the longing in her eyes?

He slid his hands into the front pockets of his pants to hide his fisted fingers. When she turned back to him, tilting her head, yearning still shadowed her gaze, and a lesser, pathetic part of him wanted to pretend that yearning was for him.

Pride insisted he not tumble down that slippery slope.

She tucked her hand into the crook of his elbow, and even though the ever-present tingle of awareness, of need, tripped over his skin, so did the soothing comfort of her touch. That calming essence that was pure…her.

"Don't let that…omen ruin your evening, Kenan. If you decide not to talk business with your father tonight, then that's your choice. And he'll have to respect it."

"Will he?" He shook his head, arching an eyebrow. "You have met Nathan Rhodes, right?"

"A time or two." She waved her glass in front of his face. "I usually reserve this for emergency situations, but if the evening calls for it, I will pull out the 'it went down the wrong windpipe and now it's triggered an asthma attack' shtick. I haven't used it since Christina Nail's wedding reception five years ago, but I'm will-ing to bite the bullet."

He widened his eyes, issuing a mock gasp. "For me?"

"Page three, paragraph six, clause A, line two of the

friendship pact demands I be willing to surrender my pride and lungs to the cause."

They looked at each other, then snickered.

"I'm almost afraid to ask what the two of you are up to," his oldest half brother, Cain, drawled as he stepped up next to them with his fiancée, Devon Cole, on his arm.

"I'm voting for no good." Devon grinned, and with her beautiful green eyes sparkling, she reminded Kenan even more of a lovely mischievous fairy than usual. "It's the only explanation why you appear to be having the most fun of everyone here."

"Behave," Cain admonished, but a smile tugged at the corners of his stern mouth—it was a miracle that most of Boston society still marveled at. Cain Farrell. Smiling. Devon Cole didn't walk on water, but she did perform other feats of wonder.

Kenan shrugged a shoulder. "She's not wrong."

"Who's not wrong?" Achilles Farrell, his other half brother—or "Jan" as Kenan called him just to irritate the bearded giant since he was the middle Farrell son—asked as he approached their group. "If it's Devon, I agree. She's right. If it's Cain, Devon's still right."

Cain shot Achilles a narrowed glare while Devon smiled at Mycah Hill—now Mycah Farrell—his wife. "You've trained him well, I see."

Mycah nodded sagely, then sipped from the glass of water Achilles handed her. Since she was nearly five months pregnant, she couldn't indulge with the rest of them. "It's all about positive reinforcement."

"Sex," Kenan stage-whispered to everyone else. "She's talking about sex."

Laughter erupted in their small group, and the knot of dread that had twisted his stomach at Gavin's announcement about their father loosened. In spite of a rocky beginning, he, Cain and Achilles had grown closer. He trusted these men—thought of them as brothers, not just half, not strangers whom he'd only found months ago.

That heaviness thickened in his chest again, pressing against his sternum as he lifted his head and found Gavin. Even if the price of that closeness with his found family had been the relationship with his adopted family.

"Kenan." Achilles hiked up his chin at him. "A minute?"

"Sure." He squeezed Eve's hand, which was resting on his elbow, then shifted to the side with his brother.

Cain nodded, indicating he would watch over Eve, and another wave of wonder uncurled inside him that now he and his brothers had evolved to unspoken communication. Shaking his head, he followed Achilles, who only moved several feet away, far enough that they could talk privately but close enough that he could keep an eye on his pregnant wife.

Kenan didn't bother stifling his snort. Just a couple of months ago, Achilles had been one of the most emotionally shut down men Kenan had ever met. Breaching a heavily guarded medieval citadel would've been easier than getting through to him. But Mycah had accomplished it. And she'd given Cain and Kenan all of their brother.

"I have some news for you," Achilles said, lifting a dark brown beer bottle to his mouth.

"Seriously?" Kenan snapped, jabbing at the beer. "Where'd you get that?"

Achilles smirked. "Jealous?"

"Hell yes."

"This—" Achilles pointed at the bottle "—is a perk of being one of the common folk attending these pretentious events. You bond with the other common folk at the bar and they hook you up." His grin flashed in his thick beard. "For once, being the Feral Farrell has its benefits."

Kenan clenched his jaw, trapping the curse threatening to escape at that fucking nickname so-called polite society had given Achilles.

"I'm kidding, Kenan." Achilles nudged him with his elbow, the blue-gray eyes that identified him, Cain and Kenan as Farrell offspring soft with understanding. "You know that shit doesn't bother me anymore. Let it go. I have."

"Yeah." Kenan rubbed a hand down his clean-shaven jaw. And he'd try. Seeing his brother so happy would help, but he still resented the hurt the people in the world Kenan lived in had caused. "So what's going on? What did you need to talk to me about?"

"It's about the search for your biological mother. You're still certain you want me to work on that, right?"

Kenan drew in a breath, held it. His pulse echoed in his head like the steady pounding of fists against a heavy bag, fierce and powerful. It vibrated through him, and when he released his breath, it trembled.

"Yes."

The answer resounded against his skull, shaking as well, but sure.

He needed to know where he'd come from, who he was. Because his brothers had been raised with their natural mothers, they possessed that very basic, vital information, but Kenan was missing that part of himself. His adoption had been closed, and regardless of his desire to know, all his life, Kenan's parents had been stubborn about keeping it that way.

But Baron's will had toppled that mandate. At least as far as his biological father. Yet, Nathan and Dana Rhodes had remained firm regarding his birth mother.

So Kenan had turned to his brother. His brother who was something of a genius when it came to computers and research.

Guilt slicked through him, as it always did whenever he considered how he'd violated his parents' wishes regarding his birth mother. Since he'd been old enough to understand the concept of adoption, he'd weighed his complicated, tangled feelings of betraying his love for Dana against his desire to know about the faceless woman who'd given birth to him.

He'd tried to bury this insatiable hunger to unearth his identity. God, he'd tried. Out of loyalty to his parents. Out of self-protection for himself. Even for the woman who'd given him up. But with the introduction of his brothers into his life...

Yeah, he had to know.

"Once you open this Pandora's box, Kenan..." Achilles studied him. Maybe this man, who saw way more than others because he spoke so much less, recognized Kenan's resolve, because he nodded. His mouth firmed. "Okay. But have you at least tried to talk to your parents about this again?"

Kenan shook his head before Achilles even finished speaking. "There's no point. They've been adamant about my biological mother not wanting to be identified or found. And they're determined to respect that. Besides they feel, rightly, that they are my parents, not the woman who abandoned me—"

"She placed you for adoption. Sacrificed to give you a better life. She did not abandon you," Achilles interrupted on a growl.

"I agree." Kenan paused, waging that aging, dusty battle of loyalty versus knowledge. "But there's no point in getting into it with them. Especially when there's nothing to tell. There *is* nothing to tell, right?" Kenan asked.

"A little more than nothing. I just needed to make sure this is what you want before I shared because there's no going back once we start." Achilles sighed. "I'm pretty sure I located the lawyer who facilitated the adoption for Baron. You already know from Baron's PI that he was aware of you and me all along and did nothing to claim us until it suited him. So your mother was free to give you up without any interference from him. And I think I found the attorney who handled that process with your parents and your biological mom. I'll do some more digging and keep you updated."

Relief, excitement and—God, he couldn't lie, not to himself—fear barreled through him, and he closed his eyes against the power of it. A big hand cupped his shoulder, the strength of it bracing him, and he leaned into it.

"It's okay," Achilles murmured. "We got you. Whatever we find."

Kenan nodded. Couldn't say anything else.

"Let's get back. Eve keeps glancing at us, and I think she's about to plan an intervention if I keep you over here any longer." Achilles squeezed his shoulder, and Kenan glanced at his brother, who cocked his head, his narrowed scrutiny almost uncomfortable. "Just out of curiosity… You plan on ever telling her you're in love with her?"

"What the hell?" Kenan's head jerked back so fast, a twinge echoed in protest at the back of his neck.

Achilles shrugged a large shoulder. "Just asking."

"You…" Kenan shook his head. Tucked his trembling hands into his tuxedo pockets. "I don't know what you're talking about."

Achilles stared at him for a long, silent, even more uncomfortable moment. Then said, "Ah." He rubbed a hand down his beard. "Sorry. I'm a people watcher."

"Damn." Kenan briefly closed his eyes. When he opened them and met his brother's sympathetic gaze, he fought not to wince. "Please don't look at me like I'm dying of an incurable disease."

"Since I was in love with a woman and didn't believe she returned those feelings just months ago, I can't help it."

In spite of the pain and humiliation punching a hole in his chest, Kenan chuckled. "That's fair." He hesitated. "Am I that obvious?"

"No." Achilles held up his hands, palms out, when Kenan tossed him an incredulous look. "I'm not lying to you. Like I said, I've spent a lifetime watching people and I was right where you are. Which is why I can ask, why not put yourself out of this particular hell? You two are best friends and from what I can see damn perfect for each other. Why not just tell her?"

A humorless smile twisted Kenan's mouth. Spoken like a man who'd found his happily-ever-after and wanted the same for everyone else. On the other side, it seemed so simple. When it was so far from it.

"Because she's in love with my brother."

"Well, fuck."

A bark of laughter slipped free at Achilles's blank, wide-eyed expression of horror. Followed by another laugh. Achilles blinked, then after a second, a chuckle rumbled out of him.

"That's screwed up."

"It is what it is." Kenan sighed, his humor disappearing as quickly as it had arrived. "Thanks, Achilles. For…"

"You're welcome."

With a dip of his chin, Kenan turned and the two of them headed back to their small group. When they reached them, Eve immediately stepped close to him, her gaze searching his. And he reached for and found the familiar mask he'd donned since he'd been a teen and realized the girl he'd called friend for most of his life had become so much more. He *wanted* so much more. He wanted *her*.

She brushed her fingers over the back of his hand. "Everything okay?"

"Fine. Just a couple of work things he wanted to go over with me." The lie rolled off his tongue. Because that was another thing he'd become proficient at over the years with her—lying. Every day he made the decision to conceal the truth, so it'd become second nature.

"Kenan," Cain said, his voice threaded with warning. "Incoming."

He hadn't needed that heads-up. Not with Eve's hand wrapping around his and squeezing. Not with the snarl of love, unease and frustration tightening inside him until he couldn't breathe past it.

Just as he'd done with Eve, he donned another mask; that was his life, after all. One for the charismatic playboy that charmed Boston society. One for the serious businessman that worked with his industry associates. Another for the wise-cracking, carefree younger brother of Cain and Achilles.

And one for the adopted son trying to prove himself worthy of being chosen by his parents.

That last mask had so many cracks and fissures from his many failures, sheer will and hope were the duct tape keeping it from falling apart.

"Mom. Dad." Kenan moved forward, greeting Nathan and Dana Rhodes as they approached. Pride and love swelled within him, temporarily eclipsing the tendrils of dread weaving through him.

Handsome and distinguished, Nathan Rhodes cut an

imposing figure through the crowd. In a ballroom full
of multibillionaires, he might not be the wealthiest, as a
mere multimillionaire, but he was definitely one of the
most respected. He helmed one of the oldest, most successful real-estate-development companies in the state,
and Rhodes Realty Inc. enjoyed a solid national reputation. Kenan's mother, beautiful and elegant, might be
one of Boston society's ruling matrons, but she also
sat on the family company's board and helped run it.

Google "power couple" and his parents didn't popu-
late just one definition, but the top three.

"Kenan." His mother extended her hands toward
him, gripping his, and drew him forward to brush
kisses over his cheeks. "You look handsome. But then,
you are my son."

He grinned and kissed her cheek. "Of course. I get
it from my mother." He turned to his father, offering
him his hand. Nathan grasped it. "Dad."

"Son. I thought you were coming by the house for
dinner before the gala. We missed you." Guilt speared
Kenan as his father's gaze flicked over his shoulder to
Cain, Achilles and their women. Nathan's eyes chilled,
then returned to Kenan. "You were probably too busy."

The guilt crystallized into diamond-bright anger—
hard, faceted and gleaming. His aversion to returning
home had everything to do with Nathan, and Kenan's
choosing not to deal with another of his father's lec-
tures about loyalty and family. He was a grown man,
yet minutes in Nathan's company could render him a
boy seeking his father's unattainable approval.

That was all on Kenan and had nothing to do with the men standing behind him.

But neither his father nor his mother would hear him on that—they wouldn't listen to him on anything having to do with Baron Farrell or his brothers. His leaving Rhodes Realty was nothing less than a defection in their eyes, an unforgivable betrayal, and the only absolution he could receive would be if he returned to the family business.

Didn't matter if his chances of advancement in his own family's company were hobbled by the mere circumstances of his birth.

Didn't matter that every contribution he made was either dissected and discarded, or grudgingly accepted then credited to another.

Didn't matter that his creativity smothered and died a slow, painful death.

All they saw was his perceived abandonment.

"Not at all," Kenan said, the same ice in his father's gaze filtering into his tone. "I just didn't have time to stop in. Which is why I promised to try instead of saying I would." He smiled, and probably shouldn't have bothered if it appeared as forced as it felt. "Of course, you two know Eve."

"Nice to see you again, Mr. and Mrs. Rhodes," Eve murmured.

"You, too, Eve." Nathan nodded.

"Eve. You look beautiful." Dana's eyes narrowed slightly. "Your mother didn't mention you were attending the gala tonight when I saw her at the office earlier."

Eve's lips twisted into a small rueful smile as she shot Kenan a sidelong glance. "It was a bit of a last-minute invite."

"Ah. I see."

Kenan waved an arm toward his brothers. "And you've met my brothers, Cain and Achilles. I'd like to introduce you to Cain's fiancée, Devon Cole, and Achilles's wife, Mycah Farrell."

Dana nodded, all warmth leeching from her expression, leaving her beautiful features cold, hard. His father didn't bother with even that small acknowledgment, and just demanded, "Can I speak to my son alone, please?"

Humiliation and fury lodged in his chest. "Dad—"

"We'll see you inside for the auction." Cain cupped his shoulder, squeezed. But the reassuring message did little to cool Kenan's temper, to assuage the pain. His brother meant to relay that they were fine, but nothing about this shit was fucking *fine*. "Sir. Mrs. Rhodes."

You don't have to go. Don't leave. Stay.

The demands, the pleas, crowded into the back of Kenan's throat. He detested how vulnerable they sounded, even in his own head. Hated more that he dreaded the thought of being alone with the two people who'd raised him.

"Kenan." Eve tugged on his hand until he tore his gaze from his father and lowered it to her. "You don't dance," she murmured. "Remember that."

Delivering the reminder of their previous conversation, she left with his brothers. Left him.

"It's not enough that you walked out on your family

business to join the company of a man who did nothing for you but donate sperm. It's not enough that you've made it clear to us that you prefer those…men you dare call brothers by not even attending dinner. But now, you're announcing that preferential treatment by publicly aligning with them over the family that took you in, raised you, when that bastard and his son wouldn't even acknowledge you until it benefited them."

"Careful, Dad," Kenan warned, stepping close to his father. *He's speaking out of anger, out of hurt.* He repeated the words to himself, but the unfairness of his father's accusations pummeled him, leaving emotional bruises that wouldn't heal as quickly as physical wounds would. "You sound very close to blaming the son for the sins of the father. And since we both know Cain is as much of a victim of Baron's manipulations as me, I can't imagine that's what you meant."

"Kenan, don't twist your father's words," his mother snapped.

"I'm not," he said, not removing his gaze from Nathan's. "I'm just clarifying. Just as I'm sure he didn't intend to imply that I've chosen anyone over my family. Unless that is what you meant, Dad."

"What's going on over here?" Gavin appeared at Nathan's elbow, his gaze shifting from their father to Kenan.

Concern darkened Gavin's brown eyes, and guilt seeped inside Kenan like water creeping through a crack. Guilt because even as Kenan loved his brother, he resented Gavin because the only woman Kenan ever wanted could only see him.

"Ask your brother. And while you're at it, ask him to define *loyalty*. From his company tonight, I think he might have forgotten that his last name is Rhodes. Maybe he wants it to be Farrell."

Pain barreled into him. Staring at his father and mother with their almond skin and dark eyes, and his brother, who was a perfect combination of their features, he'd never felt like more of an outsider. They stood, shoulder-to-shoulder, an unconscious united front against him. The adopted son with the blue-gray eyes that proclaimed him different. Announced that he wasn't…theirs.

That he didn't belong.

"Nathan," his mother said, laying a hand on her husband's arm, "please." She shot Kenan a pleading look.

"Can we not do this here?" Gavin demanded, voice low, urgent. "People are staring and talking. That's not good for us as a family, and it's not good for business. Let's table this until later. Kenan." He lifted a hand toward him. "Are you joining us for the auction?"

Kenan stepped back. "I'll see you in there," he said, not committing to it. "I'm going to refill my champagne." He held up his half-full glass, then turned and strode away before they could call him back.

He headed in the opposite direction of the room that held the charity auction. The tall double doors that led to the exit beckoned him, and he answered, shoving through to the quieter hall. Several guests milled about, but he easily skirted them to escape…

Escape.

Fuck, how he hated that word.

Didn't change what he was doing, though.

The corridor ended, and he stood in front of another set of towering doors. He briefly hesitated, then grasped the handle, opened them and slipped through to the balcony beyond. The cool April night air washed over him. The calendar proclaimed spring had arrived, but winter hadn't yet released its grasp over Boston, especially at night. But he welcomed the chilled breeze over his face, let it seep beneath the confines of his tuxedo to the hot skin below. Hoped it could cool the embers of his temper...the still burning coals of his hurt.

"For someone who is known as the playboy of Boston society, you sure will ditch a party in a hot second." Slim arms slid around him, and he closed his eyes in pain and pleasure at the petite, softly curved body pressed to his back. "All I had to do was follow the trail of longing glances from the women in the hall to figure out where you'd gone."

He snorted. "Do you lie to your mama with that mouth? There was hardly anyone out there."

"Fine," she huffed. "So I didn't go with the others and watched all of that go down with your parents and brother. I waited until you left the ballroom and went after you."

"Why?" he rasped.

He felt rather than witnessed her shrug. The same with the small kiss she pressed to the middle of his shoulder blades. He locked his muscles, forcing his head not to fall back. Ordering his throat to imprison the moan scrabbling up from his chest. Commanding his dick to stand down.

"Because you needed me," she said.

So simple. So goddamn true.

He did need her. Her friendship. Her body.

Her heart.

But since he could only have one of those, he'd take it. With a woman like her—generous, sweet, beautiful of body and spirit—even a part of her was preferable to none of her. And if he dared to profess his true feelings, that's exactly what he would be left with. None of her. Their friendship would be ruined, and she was too important to him to risk losing her.

Carefully, he turned and wrapped her in his embrace, shielding her from the night air. Convincing himself if this was all he could have of her—even if it meant Gavin or another man might have all of her—then he would be okay, he murmured, "You're really going to have to remove 'rescue best friend' off your résumé. For one, it's beginning to get too time-consuming. And two, the cape clashes with your gown."

She chuckled against his chest, tipping her head back to smile up at him. He curled his fingers against her spine, but that didn't prevent the ache to trace that sensual bottom curve.

"Where would be the fun in that? You're stuck with me, Kenan. And I'm stuck with you. Friends forever."

Friends.

The sweet sting of that knife buried between his ribs.

"Always, sweetheart."

Two

Eve smiled at the security guard as he handed her a visitor's badge in the lobby of the downtown Boston office building where Rhodes Realty occupied the fifteenth floor. She had been coming here to see her mother for so long—twenty-three years—that this place seemed like a second home, and she probably should have her own employee badge by now.

"Thanks, Mr. Leonard. Make sure you tell your wife I asked about her," she said, waving to the older man as she headed toward the bank of elevators.

"I certainly will. Take care of yourself, Ms. Eve, and have a good afternoon."

After flashing him another smile over her shoulder, she pushed the call button and, once the elevator arrived, stepped on and let it carry her to the offices of Rhodes Realty. Seconds later, she exited, and even so late on a Monday afternoon, the familiar sounds of the clatter of fingers on keyboards and the hum of conversation amid the ringing of telephones greeted her. Yet, as comforting as the soundtrack of this work environment might be, it'd never tempted her to join its ranks. No, her dream had led her in a different direction, and now she taught ninth-grade history in the Boston public-school system.

But in the last three years, that dream—her vision of her future—had changed.

Not that she could admit it to anyone.

Well, anyone other than herself and Kenan.

Always Kenan.

She couldn't contain the smile that tipped the corners of her mouth. The reaction came naturally whenever thoughts of her best friend entered her mind. This very floor had been the scene of the crime, where their friendship had started. At seven, he'd been visiting his father, her mother's new boss. And at six, she'd been stashed in the employee break room by her mother, his father's new executive assistant, because she'd been unable to find a babysitter for Eve after school. Kenan had sneaked out of his father's office and into the break-room, sneered at her Powerpuff Girls T-shirt, then offered her half his candy bar. The rest was history.

Her mother hadn't been thrilled about her friendship with her boss's son then, and nothing had changed in two decades—Yolanda Burke still disapproved. Her mother might have encouraged Eve to pursue her education, to never allow anyone to dictate her worth or her identity—she'd pushed Eve to achieve her goals and to go further than she'd been able to in her own life—but Yolanda still possessed some of her old-school beliefs. One of those was that a line existed between employer and employee, and one did not cross it. And that included the children of said employer and employee. The two worlds didn't mix.

That Eve refused to adhere to her hard-and-fast rule remained a sore point between them.

But today wasn't the day to dwell on that old argument. Not when she had great news to share.

Making her way through the labyrinthine maze of cubicles, she approached the separate set of doors that led to the executive offices. Pressing the button on the intercom, she announced herself and waited to be buzzed in. Moments later, she strode through the quieter, more expensively appointed suite. Several closed doors bore the gold plates and names of the presidents, vice presidents and senior officers of the company, including Nathan, Dana and Gavin Rhodes.

Her belly dropped, then rolled as if a fire alarm had been tripped.

Gavin.

Just the whisper of his name through her head and she reverted to being that high-school girl who'd begged Kenan to use his extra football tickets so she could watch Gavin play.

Just a glimpse of the man who could be the younger doppelgänger of actor Morris Chestnut, and the heat that danced and flickered inside her had nothing to do with girlhood and everything to do with what the woman she was wanted from him.

His touch. His love.

Hell, just his notice as someone other than his younger brother's best friend.

She sighed. Yep, she'd put that aside for now, too.

The plush, pale blue carpet silenced the fall of her heels as she approached the long circular desk that guarded Nathan Rhodes's inner sanctum. And behind the intimidating piece of furniture sat Yolanda Burke.

Love swelled in her chest at the familiar sight of her mother. And underneath, like shadows of lurking predators, swam murkier feelings. Frustration, fear. Feelings she shied away from. Feelings she hated admitted possessing.

"Hey, Mom," she greeted.

Her mother looked up from her computer monitor, smiling. And Eve stared at herself in another twenty-three years. Petite and rounded, dark brown skin, straight hair instead of natural, brown and sprinkled with gray. Eve hoped to look as youthful in her early fifties.

"Eve. When they called from downstairs to let me know you were on your way up, it was a surprise. A lovely one, though."

"I have news I wanted to give you in person. Can you take a small break?"

Yolanda glanced at her screen. "I suppose so." She pressed a couple of buttons, then rose from her chair. "I need to refill my coffee, anyway."

Eve wrinkled her nose. "Mom, really? It's four o'clock in the afternoon."

"And I still have two more hours of work to go. At least." She arched an eyebrow. "Are you forgetting I've seen you working on lesson plans at eight o'clock at night? With a travel mug of coffee when the only place you were traveling was to the kitchen table."

"All right, woman, point made," Eve grumbled, but she grinned.

"That's what I thought."

Yolanda led the way to the employee break room, and though the furniture and appliances had been updated—a one-cup coffee maker instead of the pot, a high-end refrigerator with French doors—it still remained the same room she and Kenan had spent many hours in.

"So what's this news?" her mother asked, jumping right to the point as she dropped a pod into the coffee maker.

"Well…" Eve paused dramatically, and when her mother glanced at her over her shoulder, she grinned. "I was named teacher of the year."

"Honey." Yolanda whipped around, beaming, her brown eyes glittering. Pride. Yes, pride shone there. She crossed the small space separating them and pulled Eve into a tight embrace. "Eve, that's wonderful. Congratulations. I'm so proud of you."

Closing her eyes, Eve returned the hug, inhaling her mother's no-nonsense, light-gardenia soap fragrance. The scent of her childhood. Pulling free to cup her mother's elbows, she smiled at Yolanda.

"Thank you. I'm thrilled and honored."

"You should be." Her mother squeezed her arms. "It says what your peers and administrators think about you as a teacher and person. It also shows that hard work is acknowledged. You deserve this award, Eve."

"Thanks, Mom."

That's not my only news. Not the only honor I've received.

The words loitered on her tongue as her mother patted her shoulder and returned to her coffee cup. But as much as she longed to say them, she couldn't. Couldn't tell her mother that she'd won the Small Business Award from the National Association of Women Entrepreneurs.

Because that would mean Eve would have to reveal to Yolanda that she owned a small business.

Eve smothered a sigh, guilt over her deception warring with sadness and anger for the necessity of her deceit. No, she thought, and shook her head. She could try to justify it all she wanted, but a lie was a lie. It all came down to her not having the courage to own up to the truth.

Most mothers would be delighted to discover their daughters weren't just business owners, but were wildly successful ones. But conservative Yolanda Burke, elder in her church and firm believer in all the tenets of her strict Baptist upbringing, would never support Eve being the owner and designer of Intimate Curves, an online lingerie boutique catering to plus-size women.

Not happening.

"Do you have any plans to celebrate?" her mother asked over the hiss of brewing coffee.

"Kenan offered to take me out to dinner this weekend, but that's it."

Yolanda turned once more to look at her, her dark gaze steady, sharp.

Eve just managed not to roll her eyes. She might be twenty-nine, but she wasn't crazy. "Mom. Don't."

"You're twenty-nine, Eve," she said, pretty much plucking the words from Eve's head. "You should have a boyfriend to take you out to dinner and celebrate this kind of occasion, not a—" her mouth twisted "—best friend."

"Well, I don't. And he is."

"Mr. Rhodes mentioned seeing you at the charity gala he attended with his family this weekend."

It pierced something inside Eve that even after twenty-three years of working for Nathan Rhodes, her mother still called him by his surname. Knowing Yolanda, she probably insisted on it. But still, after so long, shouldn't Nathan have demanded even more strongly that she not be so formal? They'd been together longer than some marriages, for God's sake.

Eve shook her head.

"Kenan asked me to go with him at the last minute, and I did." Eve crossed her arms over her chest, and immediately regretted the gesture. She had nothing to be defensive about. "It really wasn't worth mentioning."

"Apparently Mr. Rhodes doesn't agree." She turned around and reached for her mug, then lifted it to her mouth for a sip. "Eve, I've said it before, and regardless that you don't want to hear it, I'm going to say it again—this friendship with Kenan Rhodes isn't healthy for either one of you. He should've taken a woman he's dating or interested in dating, not you. And you should be out there looking for a man who can be a partner to you. Instead, you two are in each other's back pockets, and therefore in each other's way. I'm not the only one concerned about it. So are his parents."

What exactly did Nathan and Dana object to? That their youngest son still continued to dominate gossip columns and tabloids as Boston's most eligible bachelor and flagrant playboy, and he refused to settle down? Or that his best friend happened to be the daughter of his secretary?

How would they react if they discovered she was in love with their oldest son?

Her mother would take her name to prayer intercession then proceed to lecture her on boundaries and learning her place. There were separate worlds that coexisted—one inhabited by people like the Rhodeses and Farrells, and one for everyone else. They might work together, but they didn't mix socially, financially, geographically and definitely not romantically. Those were immutable laws, according to Yolanda Burke.

"What would you advise, Mom?" Eve quietly asked. "Cut Kenan from my life? Even when he eventually finds the woman he wants to marry, and I have a family, we'll still be friends and in each other's lives."

A curious twist wrenched her chest, and she tightened her arms. The thought of not seeing Kenan, of not confiding in him, hearing that low, wicked chuckle, or just sitting with him and letting that comforting scent of sandalwood and citrus wrap her in its familiar embrace... A dark longing yawned wide inside her, and it ached. It ached so deep she swallowed a gasp against the phantom pain.

But even more curious was the odd jerk in her belly as she mentioned Kenan falling in love and marrying another woman... Another woman who got to brush her fingertips across the sprinkle of cinnamon freckles scattered across the bridge of his nose and the high blades of his cheekbones. Another woman who was allowed to see the devilish humor light the startling beauty of his blue-gray eyes. Another woman who could curl up against that tall, lean, powerful body...

A murky swirl of emotion curdled in her belly and she scrambled away as it bubbled and hissed rather than analyze it. Heart pounding and mouth suddenly dry, she dropped her arms to her sides, mentally and physically turning away from—from herself. She strode to the window that looked over the street below, teeming with late-afternoon traffic.

"Look, Mom. I came over to share my good news with you, and to see if you had plans tonight. I wanted to treat you to dinner to celebrate, not rehash this old argument."

"Eve." Her mother's heavy sigh fell on her shoulders like a concrete shawl. One Eve had worn for so long that she barely felt its weight any longer. "I just want the best for you. And not just with your career. But for you, personally. I don't want you to be lonely."

The "like me" wasn't spoken, but it might as well as have been shouted because it echoed in the break room.

Yolanda had sacrificed so much as a single mother, had ensured that Eve remained on a path that included a stellar education, top grades and college, even steering her daughter away from her frivolous interest in art and fashion. Her mother had insisted Eve concentrate on acquiring a degree in a field where she would graduate from college and obtain a reliable, respectable job so Eve could provide for herself. So if anything happened—such as her becoming unexpectedly pregnant or a man abandoning her—she could easily take care of herself and anyone else who came along.

Her mother could've had relationships—Eve had witnessed men flirting with her—but Yolanda had remained single, focusing on work and her daughter by choice. And now, with Eve out of her home and on her own with not just one career but two—one Yolanda would consider above reproach and the other not so much—her mother was alone. And that saddened Eve. Because a woman who'd given so much deserved even more in return.

"I'm not lonely, Mom." Eve went to her mother and hugged her. "And because I don't bring anyone around you doesn't mean I don't date. Maybe they're not worthy to meet you yet. Ever think about that?"

Yolanda snorted. "Just how many of them are you seeing?"

"Tons," Eve drawled…and lied.

Because the only man she wanted didn't seem to notice she'd grown up past the age of fifteen.

"I'm praying for you."

Eve laughed, squeezing her mother's shoulders and planting a smacking kiss on her cheek.

"Abe and Louie's?"

Her mother nodded, stepping out from under her arm and lifting her coffee mug to her mouth for a sip. "You got it. Seven?"

"I'll meet you there and grab a table." She paused. "Love you, Mom."

"I love you, too, honey."

As her mother left the break room, Eve stared after her. And after watching the glass door close, she whispered, "I wish you could be proud of all of me."

Three

Cain tapped the screen on his tablet, then looked up at Kenan and Achilles, who were sitting across from him on the leather armchairs in his office's sitting area.

"That's the agenda for the board meeting next week. If there aren't any changes, I'll have Charlene finalize it and email it to everyone," Cain said, referring to his long-time executive assistant.

"Looks fine to me."

Kenan didn't have to glance at Achilles, who was older than him by a mere seven months, to see him shrug one of his massive shoulders. He didn't care much for board meetings, or meetings of any kind, for that matter. More often than not his head was buried in one of his computer programs or consumed with managing the tech company Farrell International had recently acquired to design video games geared toward at-risk youth.

"I don't think I have to remind you two that we're at six months of our—" Cain huffed out a wry chuckle "—agreement."

No, he didn't need to issue that reminder. Not to Kenan, at least.

In those six months, Cain had stepped up as the heir and successfully helmed Farrell International. He'd shown the board that although Barron had created chaos with his stunning revelation of his sons and the unorthodox stipulation in his will, he was a force of strength and stability. And Achilles, the son everyone had expected to have the most trouble acclimating to Boston and this cutthroat world of business, had discovered his niche and excelled in it.

No, it was Kenan, born into this elite world of wealth and high society, who hadn't made his mark. Who hadn't done anything of note yet. And it grated, because hadn't this been why he'd left his family's business? To not just bond with his newly discovered brothers, but to prove that he belonged here, that he could be an asset to this company, this legacy?

That he was worthy.

"I also don't think I have to tell you that our 'anniversary' will be on the minds of everyone in that meeting," Cain continued. "They'll be looking for any chink in our armor. For any hole in our solidarity."

"They can look all they want." Achilles crossed his arms over his chest. "They won't find dick."

"Ah. And they wonder who the poet is among us."

Kenan sighed, sprawling his legs out in front of him and linking his fingers over his stomach. "Are you worried, Cain? As eloquently as Achilles puts it, I have to agree."

"I'm not worried. I just…" He spread his hands wide, palms up. "Six months ago in that library, if you had told me the three of us would be here, I would've told you to stop hitting the bottle. I would've never thought…" He broke off, shaking his head. "And I damn sure know no one else believes this was possible. So I want to make sure we're all good. Consider this a check-in. Achilles?"

Achilles jerked his chin in the universal sign of "fine." When Cain arched an eyebrow in Kenan's direction, he nodded. Even as he swallowed back the urge to confess that no, he wasn't good. That he battled guilt daily for not pulling his weight in the company. For failing them.

For failing himself.

But in the end, he did what he always did. Wore another mask and said nothing.

"Good." Cain leaned back against couch. "All right, if you see any problems with the agenda, just email me, and I'll let—"

"Wait." Kenan scrolled down the screen on the tablet, his fingertip hovering over a line near the bottom of the agenda. "This item right here under 'new business.' Is this right? We're going to discuss selling Bromberg's?"

"Yes, we are."

Kenan slowly straightened in his chair, shock sliding through him like a droplet of freezing ice down his spine. "You're kidding me. They're one of the oldest, most established and well-known national department-store chains."

"And for the last three years, they've been falling in profits. It's becoming more of a financial albatross than lucrative. We have to at least discuss it. And it's likely that the board will vote to sell it."

Kenan blindly stared at the tablet, his mind shuffling through his memories and landing on the countless shopping trips to the downtown store with his mother as a kid. And then later with Eve, when they both went for prom—her for a dress and him for a tuxedo. The place claimed a special place in his memory. And the thought of it being sold and possibly disappearing under the umbrella of another company...

Excitement flickered in his chest, dancing, whirling, until it gleamed brighter. What if...? What if he could do something to save Bromberg's? This could be that opportunity he needed to prove he belonged here. That he wasn't just charming window dressing, but he brought something to the table. And he could do it by turning around a failing business. That it happened to be a business he cared about was just icing on a very profitable cake. And he could accomplish it all by doing what he did best—marketing, promotion, persuading people they wanted what he was selling.

An idea sparked like a struck match in his head, then caught flame. And it required every bit of self-control he possessed not to jump from his chair and stride out of his brother's office to get started. His heart thudded against his rib cage, pumping adrenaline in his blood like a drug.

Gripping the tablet as if it was the only thing keeping him tethered to the ground, he lifted his head and met Cain's gaze. "I have a favor to ask." When his brother dipped his chin, he said, "Could you remove the item about Bromberg's from the agenda? Just for this board meeting?"

Cain frowned. "Kenan—"

Kenan held up a hand. "I know it's a big ask, and I know it's business. But I would like time to present a proposal to revitalize the chain and turn around profits to prevent the sale. If you don't approve it, fine. But if you do, then it's possibly an opportunity to save an iconic chain and earn a profit, as well."

Several long moments passed, and Kenan held his breath as Cain studied him, his fingers steepled under his chin.

"Okay," his older brother finally murmured. "I'll have Charlene remove it from the agenda. I'm looking forward to seeing what you propose."

"I think you're going to love it," Kenan promised, smiling.

He truly believed that.

If only he could get Eve to agree.

Four

Kenan parked his black Lexus at the curb outside the brick building in Cambridge. As he switched off the ignition, he glanced at his watch. Five thirty. Eve should be home by now, and he'd called her ahead of time to make sure. Anticipation foamed inside him like a freshly poured beer, and only part of it had to do with the idea he had to present her.

Jesus.

He pinched the bridge of his nose. Dogs eager to greet their owners had more decorum than him. Just the sight of Eve's quiet, residential street, which wasn't far from both Inman Square and Union Square, had excitement humming through him, and God, how pathetic did that make him? Yeah, he refused to answer that.

Cursing under his breath, he pushed open his car

door and stepped out. He'd had so much practice at this scene, at assuming this role of platonic best friend, he slipped in and out with the blink of an eye. But by no means was it effortless. With each passing day, month, year, it required more and more…effort.

But he did it. Because losing Eve wasn't an option.

He didn't need to sit on anyone's couch to figure out his own issues and why he clung to her presence in his life. His parents had chosen him, and yet, especially with his father, he'd never felt accepted, loved without strings, without that ever-present "but."

Yes, you're a Rhodes, but not by blood.

It'd never been a secret in their household that Nathan preferred Gavin, his firstborn, natural son, the son with his DNA. Sometimes, Kenan wondered if his father regretted the adoption…or had even wanted it at all. He'd had no control in choosing his family.

But with Eve… He'd chosen her.

And she'd chosen him right back.

That had sealed both of their fates.

And, yeah, he bet his hypothetical therapist would have a field day with that.

Shaking his head, he headed up the walk to the first floor and knocked. Sliding his hands into his pockets, he impatiently waited the several moments it took for Eve to answer the door. When it opened, he braced himself. Why, he had no idea. Just pointless. Because after all these years, he hadn't managed to prepare himself for the impact of her *yet*.

And that smile.

Christ.

It lit up her face, lifting her full cheeks, and in turn, it lit up his chest. He glanced away, that smile threatening to burn down his facade as if it was a planet drawing close to the sun.

"Hey." She stepped aside, waving him in. "Come on in. You sounded so mysterious on the phone, and now I'm supercurious. Which was probably your goal."

It had been.

He entered, closing the door behind him. And as always, a sense of peace and comfort surrounded him, seeped into his skin, his bones. With the high ceilings, gleaming hardwood floors and wealth of windows throughout the wide, airy rooms, and decorated in Eve's eclectic blend of Bohemian chic meets rustic country meets thrift-store classy, her home was a haven.

He moved into the living room, taking in the nest of colorful blankets on the couch and her laptop on the coffee table next to her usual wind-down cup of peppermint tea. It was Thursday, which meant she was either working on lesson plans or updating her website with sales, new designs or any additional products she sold online at Intimate Curves, such as musk, lotions and jewelry from local merchants and artists.

She could've hired someone to maintain her website, but Eve had a bit of a problem with control. As in, she wanted all of it. Hell, it'd been a battle to convince her she needed a clothing manufacturer instead of continuing to sew her lingerie by hand. She'd argued for the personal touch; he'd countered with the creative freedom to produce more inventory. She'd said it'd be more risk; he'd come back with it meaning a bigger brand and more money.

Eventually, he'd won, and Intimate Curves, which had already been successful, had exploded. But it'd meant her loosening the reins of her control and placing that element of her business into someone else's hands. If Eve wanted, she could leave her job at the school and focus fully on the company, but she wasn't ready for that step.

Yet.

Hopefully, what he was prepared to propose would push her in that direction.

"Can you sit down? I have something I want to talk over with you." He lowered to the chair adjacent to the couch as she settled back on the couch, her gaze on him.

A small frown wrinkled her forehead as she curled a leg under her. He resolutely kept his attention on her face and not the obvious sway of her unbound breasts under her thin, dark blue hoodie, or the sexy thickness of her toned thighs revealed by the pair of faded pink-and-blue sleep shorts. Not for the first time, he wondered if she kept pieces of her inventory for herself. Imagined how those strips of lace and silk cupped her curves…molded to soft, vulnerable places he'd sacrifice every cent, every account and his damn reputation to touch, to taste, to goddamn drown in.

God. He ground his teeth together, silently and deeply inhaling through his slightly parted lips in an attempt to quell the lust wringing him tight. This might be a new low. He was fucking jealous that scraps of material enjoyed a pleasure, an honor, that he was denied.

"What's going on?" she asked, dragging his thoughts back from a place he had no business going…especially in front of her.

"Eve," he began, leaning forward and propping his forearms on his thighs, "I need you to hear me out completely before you reply or make any decision. Promise me, okay?"

Her frown deepened, but she nodded. "Okay."

He paused, let the excitement and nerves roll through him. One shot, and he needed to get this right. Eve was the linchpin of this proposal. If she said no… If he couldn't convince her, then the rest of his plan wouldn't work—

"Kenan."

He jerked up his head, not realizing until this moment that he been blindly studying her hardwood floor.

Head tilted and eyes narrowed, she studied him. "It's just me," she said softly. "Talk to me."

"Right." He exhaled. "I had a meeting with Cain and Achilles today, and we discussed the potential of selling Bromberg's department store."

"Seriously?" She shook her head, leaning back against the couch. "That place is an institution." Her gaze went over his shoulder, seeming to go unfocused. "Remember when we went shopping there for prom?" She laughed softly. "You found your tux in thirty minutes but stayed with me the two hours it took for me to pick a dress."

"I remember," he murmured. "And you're right. It

is an institution. It has history, not just here in Boston but across the nation. We're losing established businesses left and right—ones that mean something to our communities—and if I can do my part to save this one, I want to try. Cain has agreed to give me the time to come up with a proposal to present to the board."

"That's wonderful. It speaks for his confidence in you. And I'm sure whatever you come up with is bound to be amazing. You're brilliant at what you do, Kenan."

Warmth suffused him at her unconditional belief in him. Even when his family had downplayed his contributions, Eve had always encouraged him, supported him.

"Thanks, Eve. I appreciate that." He straightened and exhaled slowly. "I have an idea on how to completely rebrand and relaunch Bromberg's. It includes updating their image, retaining some of the established stores while bringing in newer, fresher clientele. My goal is to meld the classic with the modern without losing who and what Bromberg's has always represented—class, fashion and luxury. But I want to add accessibility and affordability to that without losing the luxury. That's where you come in."

She didn't speak, but he didn't miss the tension that invaded her body, stiffening her shoulders and drawing them closer to her ears.

"I want to include in my proposal an exclusive partnership with Intimate Curves."

Her full lips parted, and her sharp gasp echoed in the living room, but he pressed on. He knew Eve—knew her well. Her initial response would be a swift and emphatic "no." Fear of something new, unknown, so huge and out of her control… Whatever. He needed to work fast to make her see how this could be beneficial to both of them.

And if he needed… If it came down to it, he still had his trump card.

"You promised to hear me out before you made any decisions." He held up a hand, palm out. "Intimate Curves has fast become one of the most popular and successful online lingerie companies for plus-size women. And it's just won the Small Business Award from the National Association of Women Entrepreneurs, which is huge. But Intimate Curves is still *online*. Here is a chance to move to a brick-and-mortar store inside one of the most well-known and respected department-store chains in the nation. That would take your company to another level. It means more recognition. And exclusivity, because you can offer select designs and products in this store that aren't available anywhere else. Which means more profits. It would also bring a fresher, more modern, woman-positive image to the chain. And, of course, we're not even touching on what Intimate Curves does for size and sex positivity overall."

He rose, the pulses of excitement too much for him to remain seated. It got like this for him when a new project started forming. He vacillated between extreme focus and bouncing around like a kid on a sugar high. Right now, he paced the length of the room, striding over to her built-in bookshelves crammed with everything from texts on ancient Roman emperors, to the

Civil War, to her favorite romance books. Then, he whirled around and ate up the distance to the massive fireplace on the other wall.

"Kenan." Eve released a short chuckle that carried a note of disbelief, and when he glanced at her, she stared at him, her hands fluttering in front of her. "I have no idea what to say here. Other than what the hell do you want me to say to that?"

"Say yes, Eve. Say *yes*."

Okay, so he couldn't hide the desperation in his voice. But then again this was Eve, so he didn't try. There was no point, anyway. She could ferret out every one of his emotions, every hint of a deception. Unless it pertained to her, that is. It seemed when it came to her, he was a fucking master of illusion.

"What is this really about, babe?" she quietly asked.

Shit.

He nearly winced. Nearly. And he *nearly* confessed the truth to her. But there were some things he couldn't even admit to his best friend. Well, other than the obvious. He couldn't tell her that he *needed* this. He needed to prove to the board, to his brothers, to his family—to his goddamn self—that he'd made the right decision in leaving Rhodes Realty. That incurring his parents' anger and disappointment hadn't been in vain. That he was worthy of being at Farrell International.

That he was worthy of being a Farrell.

He despised the weakness in himself for even thinking that last one.

Hated even more that he meant it.

"I know you enjoy teaching, Eve," he said, walking

over to the couch and lowering down beside her. He met her beautiful brown eyes, saw the shadows of uncertainty in them. He hungered to reach for her, curl his hand behind her neck and draw her into his body. Offer himself as a resting place, a haven. But that's not what she needed from him. Not now. "But you *love* creating, designing. You're never more alive than when you're sketching out a new creation. You even crave the challenge of running your own business, of besting your own self every month when those numbers come in. This—" he jabbed a finger at her laptop with the Intimate Curves logo on the screen "—is what you should be doing full-time. If you would just take that leap of faith."

"That's easy for you to say." She glanced away from him, thrusting her fingers into her thick curls, fisting them.

"Is it?"

She flinched. "Shit. I'm sorry, Kenan. I didn't think."

"Doesn't matter." He waved off her apology. "Tell me your objections."

"You know them." She sighed, and the weariness in the sound settled on his chest like two-ton weight. "They haven't changed. Even while I'm so damn proud of this award, do you know what one of my first thoughts was while reading the email? 'I hope I won't have to accept anything in person.' The idea of Mom and the school finding out? Jesus." She shook her head, letting loose a dry laugh. "I'm twenty-damn-nine. Too old to be worried what my mother is going to say about my life choices, and yet—" she stretched her arms wide, her fingertips grazing his arm "—here I am," she drawled. "Rationally, I recognize I can't live my life for her, but seeing that disappointment on her face when she's done so much for me, sacrificed so much…"

"Yes, but for how much longer? Until next year? And then until you're thirty-five? Forty? When is enough, enough? When do your dreams become more important than someone else's comfort?"

She parted her lips and was about to reply…but no answer came. He didn't need one. He spied the yearning for what he described in her eyes.

"Six designs. Six Eve Burke designs exclusive to Bromberg's that I can promise will roll out with the relaunch. Just give me that commitment. I'm looking at six to eight months for this, so you have that long to determine how much you'd want to be involved beyond the stores. I can find a team to manage the store division, so if you're adamant about protecting your identity, continuing to teach and focusing on the online arm of the company, then that's an option for you." He paused. "I have another offer."

She arched an eyebrow. "I'm almost afraid to ask."

He didn't smile at the teasing note in her voice, though. Not when tiny razor blades left him so wounded by the offer it was a wonder he could still sit upright on her couch.

"If you agree to my proposal, I'll help you with my brother."

Fuck, those words scalded his throat, his tongue. Even as he said them, part of him roared that he should rescind them. But he didn't. And they hung between him and Eve like ripe fruit on a vine that she was probably dying to pick.

And damn if another part of him didn't resent her for that, too.

She blinked. Stared at him. "What the hell are you talking about?"

His mouth twisted into a wry half smile. "I'm talking about Gavin, served up on a platter. Or maybe you serving yourself up on a platter to him. I don't know how you prefer it. Equal opportunity and all that shit. Doesn't matter. I've spent thirty years with him. I know him better than anyone. Understand what grabs his attention in a woman. I love you, Eve, but your flirtation game when it comes to him is woefully inadequate. You want an 'in' with him, I'll give it to you. I can't promise you you'll be the next Mrs. Rhodes—" *fuck me* "—but with me as your…love coach, you'll have a chance."

"Love coach?" she sneered. "Are you serious right now? If you could've helped me with your brother, why are you just doling out these jewels of wisdom now? Why not before?"

Because I didn't want him to have you before. Not when I still held a delusional hope that I could.

But he no longer held that fantasy. At some point, between leaving Cain's office and driving over to her Cambridge apartment, he'd come to a hard but final decision.

Eve didn't want him. She never had.

It'd always been Gavin for her.

So he had to let go of the dream of her.

No matter how it hurt.

Not the friendship; never that. But he was giving up the fantasy of ever being more. For fifteen years, he'd secretly loved and lusted after a person who had only seen him as a friend—or worse, a brother. He had to face reality, and not waste another year, another month, another damn day on a fruitless wish. Besides, if by some miracle, Eve actually returned his feelings, he would always question if she was settling for him because she couldn't have Gavin.

He'd been second best all his life. Being that for Eve? His gut twisted with a howl of pain. Jesus, no. Not with her.

What he could do, though, was pour all of himself into this vision of his future. And in doing so, he could help his friend obtain her own dreams—the career of her heart and his brother.

And in return, he'd cement his place in Farrell International, proving he was more than Barron's bastard. He'd prove he was needed and that he belonged there.

It would have to be enough.

Even if right now it didn't feel like it.

"Because you never asked me before. And I'm a self-serving son of a bitch, and it benefits me to hook you up with him now." It was a lie, but with just enough of a grain of truth that she might go for it.

Please go for it, Eve. I can't emotionally afford for you to dig deeper.

She tilted her head, eyes narrowing on him.

"So let me get this straight. I give you six designs—"

"Exclusive designs for an Intimate Curves flagship store in Bromberg's."

She paused. "I give you six exclusive designs with the extent of my involvement in a flagship Intimate Curves store to be discussed at a later date, and besides a partnership agreement, you will coach me in how to win the attention and affection of your brother."

"Yes."

"Why?" she whispered.

If she hadn't asked with that note of insecurity and pain in her voice, he might have deflected with a flippant answer. Instead, he thumbed a big "fuck you" at his control, leaned forward and cupped her cheek. He shoved, not nudged, the friendship boundary, and brushed his thumb under the curve of her bottom lip. Back and forth. Back and forth. Until the need to trace that path with his tongue became an all-too-real urge and he stopped.

"What are you asking me, Eve? Why am I helping you? Or why do I think Gavin will want you?"

"Either." A pause. "Both."

Yes, he'd decided to move on, to let her go, but that didn't mean the streak of masochism had disappeared. Only that could explain why he tunneled his fingers into her dark brown curls, their rough-silk texture dragging a groan from deep in his gut. Only by sheer force of will did he lock it down. But nothing could keep him from imagining it grazing his bare chest, his stomach… his thighs. Could stop him from envisioning his hands buried in it up to the wrists, holding the mass of it away from her face as she took him…

Damn…

Sweat broke out on the back of his neck. He dropped his arms, flattening his hands on his legs, hiding the prickling of perspiration on his palms.

She'd asked him a question. About his brother. The man she wanted. The man she'd always wanted.

Not you. Never you.

He jackknifed from the couch and stalked over to the window, staring out onto her quiet street and the gathering shadows. With his back to her, he could affix his mask and hide the erection thrusting against his zipper from just having touched her hair, as if demanding her hand, her attention.

He closed his eyes. "I'm helping you because you deserve every happiness, every desire, every goal—you deserve everything, Eve. Not that you didn't before. But maybe it was me being selfish then. Not wanting to share you. And this is me realizing I can't do that. Holding you back is holding me back, too. I meant what I said. Your dimmed light shouldn't be at the cost of someone's comfort. And that includes mine." Wasn't that the fucking truth? Bitterness coated his throat, burned in his veins like corrosive acid. "As for Gavin." He turned around, sliding his hands in his pants pockets. "My brother might not have noticed the beauty right under his nose, but that's not your fault. It's all on him. He's a fucking idiot. Worse. A blind fucking idiot. But if that's who you want, I'll help you grab his attention. He won't know what hit him, sweetheart."

She inhaled a deep breath, slowly exhaled it. Then she stood and crossed the room, approaching him. He resolutely kept his gaze on her face, as he'd done earlier. And so he noted the acceptance there before she extended her hand toward him.

Loss shouldn't have wrapped around his throat and squeezed. Shouldn't have filled his nostrils, sat heavy on his tongue until the acrid flavor was all he smelled, tasted.

She stood right there, her small, dainty palm pressed to his. Her chocolate gaze smiling into his. And, yet, he couldn't get rid of the sense that things had changed for them with the excitement in her eyes. The excitement and the agreement.

"Okay, I accept. Let's do this."

"We have a deal then."

He shook her hand.

Sealing both of their fates.

Five

Eve stood on the sidewalk outside the hair salon and scanned Dorchester Avenue for a glimpse of the familiar black Lexus through the heavy foot traffic.

On a late Saturday morning, near the riverfront and with Fenway Park not far away, people teemed outside, enjoying the unusually warm spring day. And by unusual, she meant sixty degrees. Didn't stop people from wearing everything from sweaters to shorts as they strolled in and out of the book café next to the hair salon, or the tattoo shop and restaurants along the street. Already, music was pouring from some of the bars. Some people bought and enjoyed fresh lemonade from the cart parked on the walkway. To a tourist, it probably seemed like a big block party, but no. This was just…Boston.

She glanced down at her watch, impatience streaking through her. No, not impatience. Well, maybe just a little. But mostly, nerves. Because she was doing this. Taking this step. Making a change she'd been contemplating for a while but had been hesitant about doing because… There were so many reasons. Now, in the week and two days since Kenan had arrived at her house and presented his proposal, those reasons had gradually altered in her head, becoming excuses. And they all boiled down to one thing…

Fear.

For God hath not given us the spirit of fear; but of power, and of love, and of a sound mind.

Second Timothy, chapter one, verse seven.

One of her mother's favorite scriptures. When Eve had been terrified about standing up in front of her class to deliver her first speech on Crispus Attucks in history class in the fifth grade, Yolanda had quoted that verse. When Eve had confessed the night before she'd left for college that she was afraid to leave home for the first time, her mother had whispered the same passage in her ear, while hugging her close, tears thick in her voice.

When Eve had called her mother from her car on her first day as a teacher, scared as hell of walking into that high school, her mother had reminded her of this scripture.

It seemed kind of sacrilegious to murmur the verse to herself now, when she was praying over gathering the courage to pursue a man who had shown zero interest in her beyond that of acknowledging her existence.

But what was the scripture about God giving her the desires of her heart?

Oh, Lord, she was going to hell.

"Eve."

The sound of her name and the touch at her elbow jerked her from her thoughts of imminent damnation. She glanced up at Kenan, who arched an eyebrow. Rather than answer, she ruefully shook her head.

"Hey." Lifting her cell phone, she tapped the screen. "You're late."

Showing a marked lack of remorse, he shrugged a cream, cable-knit-covered shoulder. "Since you didn't deem it important to share what I'm late for…"

"Does it ma—"

She narrowed her eyes, really *seeing* him. As in the five-o'clock shadow that ticked closer toward six, since it didn't appear as if he'd shaved since the night before. It'd been a week since they'd seen each other—the longest they'd gone without being in each other's company since college. Silky, light brown hair dusted the sensual bow of his upper lip and a small patch dotted the dip beneath the almost ridiculously full bottom curve.

Either he'd been burning the candle at both ends, which was definitely a possibility, given she didn't know anyone who worked harder than him. Or… Or, he'd just rolled out of a woman's bed and hadn't taken the time to go home and shave but had come straight to Eve. Another distinct possibility. Because as hard as Kenan worked, he played equally as hard.

If she leaned in, would she catch a whiff of the other woman's perfume or the musk of their sex on his skin?

A blaze, like a hundred fire ants, streamed through her, rippling across her scalp and down her spine, before reversing course and pouring into her chest. Her breath caught, and that went up in smoke under the flames of... Of what? Anger? Yes, but it didn't feel as...clean, as simple as that. But she refused to latch onto the other word her mind seemed so eager to supply. No. This was stupid, silly. Why did she care who Kenan fucked? She *didn't*. It wasn't her business. Never had been.

Then why are you squeezing your phone so hard? The address book is going to be imprinted on your palm.

Deliberately, she loosened her grip.

"Does what matter?" He cocked his head.

"Nothing." She waved a hand. "So the reason I asked you down here..." She turned and looked at the beauty salon in back of her. "I've scheduled a makeover."

He stared at her. "A what?" he asked, voice low. Almost...menacing.

She shivered.

Then ignored it. She was being ridiculous.

"A makeover," she repeated. When he didn't say anything more, just continued to stare at her with that unblinking, bright stare, she stumbled on, even though she didn't owe him an explanation. "Look, I can practically see what you're thinking. And, no, I'm not changing for a man."

"No?" He crossed his arms. "Then what do you call it?"

"Changing for me." She tapped her fingertips to the middle of her chest. "I've been thinking about this for a while. Don't do that," she snapped, when his full lips pressed into a thin line. "I'm not lying. There are things I've wanted to change. My hair." She reached up, touched the ends of her thick spirals, then dropped her hand and glanced down at her form-fitting but plain green V-neck sweater and dark blue skinny jeans. "My clothes. I want...different."

She wanted to stand out. To be noticed. When she entered a room, she wanted men to stop in midsentence because they forgot their train of thought, and women to glare in envy.

Was that so wrong? Shallow maybe, but wrong?

Possibly, but at this moment? She didn't care.

"And you just now decided to do something about it? Out of the blue," Kenan drawled, skepticism dripping from his tone like condensation from one of those cups of cold lemonade.

"I know what you're getting at, and so what?" She threw her hands up between them. "Your proposal about Gavin might have been the push I needed, but he isn't the reason. Why can't this be about me?" she demanded, frustrated and more than a little annoyed. "Of course, *you* wouldn't understand that."

He frowned, slowly loosening his arms and lowering them to his sides. "What the hell is that supposed to mean?"

"Please, Kenan. You have a mirror. And even if that wasn't enough of a clue, the women climbing all over you would be another one. You don't know what it is to be…invisible."

"And you do?" He studied her, that blue-gray gaze roaming her face so intently she stifled the urge to duck her head, hide from him. And that wasn't them. They didn't hide anything from each other. "You could never be invisible, Eve. Not even if you tried."

"Spoken like a true friend." She shook her head, briefly smiling. "But also spoken like someone who's never had cause to doubt his own beauty or appeal in his life."

Something bleak, almost…desolate flashed in his eyes before the thick fringes of his lashes lowered. What the hell? She reached for him, her fingers grazing the inside of his wrist, but he stepped back, scrubbing his hand over his head. It shouldn't have felt like rejection.

But it did.

"You dead set on this?" he demanded, voice hard, low.

A bolt of nerves attacked her, striking her and leaving her trembling. But it was that fear of change, of the unknown, that affirmed she was doing the right thing. She'd experienced this same feeling when she'd decided to secretly minor in fashion. And when she'd opened Intimate Curves. And, most recently, when she'd agreed to Kenan's proposal.

It hadn't served her wrong yet.

"Yes."

With one last, long stare, he pulled his cell out of his pocket and strode away from her. Curiosity and impatience warred for dominance within her, and she glanced down at the screen of her own phone. Her appointment was in fifteen minutes. She'd called him for moral support, but she wouldn't allow him to make her late.

A few minutes later, she took a step toward the shop when he turned and stalked back toward her.

"C'mon." He jerked his head, grasping her elbow.

"What?" Too shocked to disobey his command, she fell into step beside him, but then gathered the lady balls she'd temporarily misplaced. "Hold up." She abruptly skidded to a halt, jerking her arm free of his hold.

"At some point in the last five minutes you suddenly mistook me for a sheep. I don't know how that happened, but I'm going to offer you the benefit of the doubt since we're lifelong buddies. So let's try this again. What's going on and where are you trying to haul me off to?"

Kenan sighed. "If you're determined to go through with his crazy-ass idea, then I have a connection who hooked me up with a full-service salon in the Back Bay. Private, high-end, with a stylist and makeup artist. But we have to leave right now."

He shifted closer. Then closer still, completely invading her personal space with his scent, his body. All of *him*.

"But this needs to be said, Eve. You're perfect. Just as you are. I promised to help you get Gavin's attention by teaching you how to flirt with him, tease him. Not by changing yourself. You don't need to do that for him or any man. I know." He jerked up his chin when she parted her lips to object. "I heard you. This is for you. I'm just reiterating. There's no need for it. But this is your decision, and I'll support it. But, Eve, this…"

His hand thrust in her hair, his blunt nails scraping over her scalp before he fisted her curls. Her breath caught in her throat, and she barely jailed her whimper before it escaped. The needy sound that echoed in her head sent shock crackling within her like a live wire. Shock and something darker…hungrier… That *something* shivered through her, setting off tiny ripples that pooled low in her belly.

No. This is Kenan, she reminded herself. *My best friend.*

She blinked up at him, her hands coming to rest on his chest. Was she pushing him back or needing to feel his strength against her palms?

God. Why couldn't she answer that?

"This, Eve." He tugged on her hair, the pleasurable prickles dancing across her scalp—another sensory overload adding to the confusion coalescing inside her. "This you're not changing." He lifted the strands still clutched in his fist to his nose, and in doing so, drew her forward until her forehead brushed his lips, and she had no choice but to inhale the sandalwood and citrus scent of him from the cradle of his throat. "This is mine."

This is mine.

Shit.

This was where she should open her mouth and protest. Tell him he was not her owner or her keeper. That she could make her own decisions about her hair, thank you very much. But she didn't. Not with that possessive declaration of "this is mine" echoing in her head—and between her legs—like a molten heartbeat.

"Where are we going again?" she whispered.

For a long moment, he didn't speak or release her. But then he shifted backward, his grip on her curls loosening.

"I told you, a place recommended by a friend. Now, where are you parked? I'll go get my car so you can follow me to my place. We'll drop your car off there, and you can ride to the salon with me."

"A friend?"

Like the friend he'd most likely left limp, tangled in sheets and smelling like him and the sex they'd had all night?

Okay, she really had to get a grip. From twelve to fourteen, she'd had a secret crush on Kenan. If these thoughts skidding through her head had happened then—well, obviously not the *sex*, but this inexplicable cattiness and…to hell with it, jealousy—that would make sense. But that was then, not now.

So yeah, she had to get it together. Because again, *best friend.*

"Yes, a friend. Mycah."

"Oh, right." Heat tinged her cheeks, as an image of Achilles's wife flickered in her head. She boasted gorgeous natural curls, just as Eve did. Dammit, she really needed to just shut up. "I'm parked down there." She pointed toward the other end of the street. "I'll just meet you at your house."

Without waiting for his agreement, she turned and strode off. Time by herself. That's what she needed. Time to calm her nerves, get centered. Cancel her original appointment and make Kenan paid the fee since, technically, he was responsible for the cancellation. And then, maybe she needed to examine the dregs of that morning coffee. Because there must've been something extremely funky in the cup she'd grabbed this morning. Nothing else explained her responses to Kenan in the last few minutes.

Or the tight ache pulsing deep inside her.

Good. God.

"I—I'm—" Eve stared at herself in the mounted, lighted mirror in the hair salon. She shook her head in disbelief, her newly winged eyes wide.

Her contemplation shifted to the smiling woman behind her.

"You're you." Jasmine, her stylist, fluffed Eve's curls, then settled her slender hands on Eve's shoulders. "Gorgeous. All we did was bring a little glamour to you. That's all."

"I think you're really underselling your skill, but okay," Eve drawled, still unable to stop staring at her reflection. At the woman with the flawless makeup and hair gazing back at her.

Jasmine chuckled, whipping the cape off her. "Trust me when I tell you I've worked with more…difficult clients. You, Eve, are not one of them. Come on to the front. I have a bag of products for you to take home with you."

"Do you have a three-page, single-space essay and video tutorial to go along with it? Because as gorgeous as you made me, I'm experiencing serious doubts if I can recreate this at home."

Laughing, Jasmine led her from her private room, which Eve had learned earlier she reserved for her VIP clients. Eve Burke. A VIP client. When did she step through the wardrobe and why did she have to go back to the real world?

In the three and a half hours she'd been at the exclusive Back Bay salon, Jasmine and her team had completely pampered her. Hair, a facial, makeup, manicure and pedicure. She'd never been so catered to and spoiled in her life. Growing up, extra splurging money had been a concept she'd heard of, not a real thing. And, as an adult, even though she held down a full-time job as a teacher and ran a successful company that turned a decent profit, she still wrestled with guilt.

Watching her mother squirrel away money to make sure Eve didn't go without necessities had branded an impression on her that Eve couldn't remove. Spending money on a new spring wardrobe when she could put aside extra money just in case her car broke down, or she lost her job, seemed selfish. Shelling out money on a spa day or a vacation when she could pour that back into her business was irresponsible.

Frivolous. The word whispered in her head, and it was her mother's no-nonsense voice. Yolanda had deemed several things frivolous. Eve's friendship with Kenan. Her wanting to try out for the school dance team. Her wanting the newest cell phone.

Her love of art and drawing…

God. Eve shook her head, focusing on Jasmine's retreating back. How had she gone down that morose rabbit hole? Nope. There was no room for glum thoughts today. Not when she'd taken the first concrete steps toward becoming her best self. The one she'd been scared of being for so long.

Because that meant putting herself out there. Being seen. Being potentially criticized. Being potentially rejected…

Okay, for the love of all that's holy, stop*!*

She stepped out into the waiting area, scanning the room decorated in black, white and chrome. Two couches, several chairs and tables filled the space, and gilded mirrors adorned the walls, along with several framed photographs of gorgeous women modeling different stunning hairstyles.

Kenan was perched on one of the armchairs, his phone in hand, attention centered on the screen. But, as if he sensed her, his head lifted, that focused, bright gaze finding her. His eyes flared wide then narrowed as he slowly rose to his feet.

Eve battled the impulse to touch her face, her hair, to fidget under that intense, hooded perusal. Its weight settled on her. But it wasn't suffocating. Oh, no, not that. That gaze moved over her like a lover shifting between her legs, the solid bulk pressing into her body. Branding her. Heat, scalding and strong, like undistilled liquor, shot through her. Tingled in her breasts, beaded her nipples. Burned in her belly. Spasmed in her sex.

What. In the. *Hell?*

She stumbled, grasping the edge of the counter. This couldn't be—she didn't want Kenan. Not sexually. It'd always been Gavin. Maybe that's what…this was. The prospect of being on the precipice of having the chance to be with the man she'd desired for so long must be messing with her head…and other lady parts. Because, admittedly, it'd been a long while since a man had touched her. Covered her. Slid so deep inside her she couldn't breathe past that sense of fullness.

Yes, that had to be why one look from her best friend had her tangling with lust like a sordid game of Twister.

"Here you go, Eve." Jasmine handed her a black-and-white bag with pink accents. "Everything you need, and some extrafun things I threw in for you. And if you have any questions, please don't hesitate to call me. I included my card in here, as well."

"Thank you so much, Jasmine." Eve accepted the bag and, on impulse, hugged the other woman. "You have no idea how much I appreciate all you've done. How much do I owe you?"

"No worries." Jasmine waved off her question as Eve reached for the wallet in her purse. Eve paused, frowning at the stylist. "It's been taken care of."

Oh, she didn't need to ask by whom.

Saying goodbye one last time, Eve walked into the waiting area and approached a silent, frozen Kenan. He didn't blink, didn't budge, and that antsy, fidgety feeling returned.

"What?" She lifted a hand toward her hair but halted

at the last second. "I didn't change my hair. She just gave me highlights."

He still didn't say anything. Just stared. And, dammit, it was seriously starting to unnerve her.

She knew what he saw. Jasmine had washed, conditioned and moisturized her hair, and the curls, with their new red highlights, gleamed and framed her face, grazing her shoulders. The makeup artist had given her a full day look and her eyes had never appeared so wide, her cheekbones so high, her lips, painted a beautiful deep bronze, so full.

"Are you happy?"

She lifted her shoulder in a small, half shrug, accompanying the gesture with a slightly nervous laugh.

"Jasmine did a wonderful job."

"That doesn't answer my question. Are you happy?"

"Yes." This was what she wanted. A new look. A new beginning. A new *her* as she started this journey to putting aside fear, maybe becoming the face of her company and going after the man she'd desired for years. "Yes," she said again, firmer this time.

He studied her for a long moment, and for the second time in the history of their long friendship, she wanted to hide from that all-too-perceptive gaze.

"Okay." He nodded. "C'mon. We have another appointment."

Kenan turned, heading toward the salon's exit.

"Wait." She grabbed his arm, annoyance rippling through her. "What appointment? And that's it? That's all I get, is an 'are you happy?'"

"A clothing boutique. Someone is going to meet us there."

She shouldn't be offended. After all, this makeover had been her idea. But, damn, did he have to jump so fully on board?

"Look at me."

She jerked up her head, not realizing until then that she'd dropped her gaze and was scanning her completely fine but plain clothes.

"There's nothing wrong with the way you dress. The way you look. The way you fucking *breathe*, Eve. But if I'm going to hold up my end of the bargain, that means attending certain events where Gavin will be. And you need the wardrobe to attend them. No." He held up his hand, preventing the objection that she'd definitely been prepared to make. "This is my bargain. Consider it a business expense."

Once more, he pivoted on his heel and headed for the door. Just as his hand closed around the handle, he paused. "And you're stunning."

Eve stared. Even after he pushed through the door and it closed behind him, she remained rooted to the spot inside the salon.

There's nothing wrong with the way you dress. The way you look. The way you fucking breathe, *Eve.*

You're stunning.

His words played through her head in a continuous loop. Her breath shuddered out from between her lips, and she pressed a palm to her belly, as if the gesture could quell the quivering there.

It didn't.

Shaking her head, she exhaled a deep breath that ended on a dry, disbelieving chuckle.

She really needed to get her head on straight. Today might be like some reverse Cinderella story, but nowhere in that fairy tale did she fall in lust with her best friend.

This was not that kind of story.

Six

"Remind me why I'm here again? On a school night?" Eve muttered.

"I'm sorry. Did I miss the memo where you turn into a pumpkin at midnight? Or a lesson planner?"

Eve snorted. "Very funny. Ass."

Kenan smirked, murmuring a thank-you to the bottle-service waitress as she set vodka and Patrón tequila on the table in front of him and Eve, along with glasses, cranberry juice and a bucket of ice. She smiled at him, and he recognized and acknowledged the invitation in it with a dip of his chin. Not that he'd do anything about it.

Tonight wasn't about him.

It was about the woman sitting next to him on the dark red leather couch in the VIP section of The Trend, the new nightclub in the seaport district his brother had invested in. Gavin had invited Kenan to the opening, and he'd brought Eve along as his plus-one. Tonight he would start to uphold his end of the bargain.

Shit.

He might need to call back their waitress for more liquor if he was going to make it through this night. A night of not only having a ringside seat to Eve pursuing his brother, but Kenan also helping her to catch him.

Leaning forward, he grabbed the bottle of vodka and poured a healthy amount in a glass, forgoing the cranberry juice. He tilted the drink up to his mouth and shot it back. The burn razed a path down his throat, and he savored it. Concentrated on it. Because if he focused on that burn, then he could shift his attention away from the one that clawed at his gut and hardened his cock.

Jesus.

He moved his gaze away from her. The tangible, sexual *lure* of her.

He could take his eyes off her, but the picture of her was branded into his mind—that petite, curvy body poured into tight, black leather pants, a white, high-collared silk shirt with a feminine bow at the throat and ankle boots with "fuck me hard" stiletto heels.

She was sex and innocence. Sin and sweetness. A walking, breathing temptation in leather, silk and flesh.

Gavin wouldn't be able to resist her.

And Kenan had no one to blame but himself.

He poured another drink. Tequila this time.

"Whoa there. The evening is just getting started,"

Eve cautioned with an arched eyebrow. "Everything okay?"

"Fine." He poured her a vodka-and-cranberry and passed it to her. "Here. Catch up." He waited until she lifted the drink to her mouth and sipped, then clasped her hand in his and brought her to her feet. And turned away. Because, Jesus. Those hips and that ass. "Come on. Let's go do what we're here for."

The sooner he started this lesson in how to reel in his brother, the sooner he could start getting down to the serious business of drowning his brain in alcohol. He'd need it to stop seeing the images of Eve and Gavin twisted together, kissing and touching. Besides, if he was drunk, he wouldn't be sober enough to swing on his brother for taking what Kenan coveted.

"I can't believe your brother is an investor in this place." She held on to him, allowing him to guide her down the steps from the glass-enclosed VIP section to the bar and club section below. "It's amazing."

Kenan clenched his jaw at the awe and admiration coating her voice. All his life, he'd stared at the pedestal on which his parents had placed Gavin. Watching Eve worship at that same throne?

Alcohol.

Sooner rather than later.

He needed something to wash down the bitter flavor of envy.

As soon as the bouncer opened the door to the club, the muted, thumping bass and music that had vibrated off the glass of the VIP section bombarded them. Hundreds of people packed the grand nightclub that reminded him of a Vegas venue. Aside from the luxurious VIP lounges, a dual spiral staircase that wouldn't have been out of place in an English palace led to a second story, where a DJ spun her beats and more people danced on the landings and catwalks. Below, three bars, two huge dance floors and several scattered sitting areas filled with tables, chairs and booths encompassed the cavernous space. A lighting system flashed gold, green and white beams, while two LED walls played music videos.

If tonight's attendance was any indication, Gavin had made a sound investment. Kenan was happy for him.

Speaking of Gavin...

His brother stood at the end of the longest bar, surrounded by a group of men and women vying for his attention. Instead of heading over to him, Kenan steered Eve to the opposite end, sliding up to the bar top and shielding her with his body.

"Shouldn't we go talk to Gavin? Say hi?" Eve rose on her tiptoes, her lips brushing the rim of his ear. Even in those ridiculously high heels she remained several inches shorter than him. "He probably doesn't know we're here..."

"He knows we're here. It was his name and connections that granted us access to the VIP section."

Kenan slid an arm around her waist, his fingers splaying wide over the sexy, rounded curve of her hip. Her soft gasp puffed against his cheek as her chest met his, and he pulled her to stand closer between his legs. Cedarwood and roses greeted him, and he battled the urge to bury his face in the crook between her shoulder and neck, and inhale more of her delicious, skin-warmed scent.

"Kenan," she whispered, gripping his arms.

"Shh. Lesson number one, Eve." He pinched her chin, tilting her head back and to the side so that her breath ghosted across his mouth. Damn, he hungered to lick his lips, taste her in the only way he could. "You don't chase after anyone. Let them do the pursuing."

She scoffed, but he caught the slight tremble in her voice. The uncertainty. "Isn't that what I'm doing here? Pursuing?"

"No. I'm teaching you how to make the one you want work for you. Now…" He bowed his head, his lips skimming over her cheek, hovering just above her ear. Because he could, under the guise of pretense, he tangled the fingers of his free hand in her hair, fisting the curls. "Gavin is used to people—women—chasing him, currying favor with him, throwing themselves at him. And while he doesn't duck and dodge, he doesn't experience the thrill of the chase. Every man craves that thrill, the excitement of it. The challenge of it. The arousal of the takedown and the conquering."

"God, Kenan. You make him sound like an animal." She chuckled, and it sounded breathless. His grip on her hip tightened before he deliberately eased it. That wasn't for him; that telltale signal of excitement belonged to the idea of being captured and covered by his brother. *Don't get it fucking twisted.*

"That's what we are, sweetheart. At the core, we're beasts who convince ourselves we're predators. But the truth? The truth is—our secret—we're your prey all along, and we love every goddamn moment of being taken by you."

"Kenan." Her lashes fluttered, and her fingers flexed against his arms.

Suddenly, he knew with crystal clear certainty how she would cling to him during sex. Knew the exact pressure her nails would exert against his skin, his muscles. Lust beat at him with merciless fists, and he delighted in being its punching bag, even acknowledging he couldn't do a damn thing about it.

"Kenan." A new voice—deeper, lower and familiar—intruded, dousing Kenan with a brutal, icy dose of reality. Forcing a casual smile, he untangled his fingers from her hair, but kept his arm around her waist as he turned them to face his brother.

"Hey, man," Gavin said. "Thank you for coming out tonight."

Gavin pounded Kenan on the shoulder in greeting. His curious and, goddammit, admiring gaze slid to Eve and lingered on her. Roamed over her face, pausing on her lush mouth before dipping lower to her equally lush body. Anger, pain, jealousy—they all roared inside Kenan, pounded against his bones, rattling him from the inside out.

But he kept his mask in place. This time, it was one that showed him as the carefree, "rejection rolls right off my back" younger brother.

Fortunately, he was well versed in maintaining this facade.

"Of course. I wouldn't miss it," Kenan said with a

wide grin, clapping his brother on the shoulder in return. "Since you said I could bring a guest, I convinced Eve to tag along."

"I'm glad you did." Gavin turned to Eve, and instead of the usual polite but distant smile, this one held an appreciative warmth that reflected in his dark eyes. "Eve, it's good to see you again. You look…stunning," he said, his voice lowering, deepening.

"Thank you, Gavin," she murmured, and even in the darkness of the club, Kenan glimpsed the flush across her cheekbones. Or maybe he just knew her so well, he could picture it there. "Congratulations, by the way. I was just telling Kenan how amazing the club is."

"I appreciate it. A lot of hard work went into renovating it." He cocked his head to the side, a corner of his mouth quirking. "How about you two join me? I was about to head up to our VIP section with my partners and a few guests. I'd love if you two—" he glanced at Kenan, then quickly returned his gaze to Eve "—would come with us."

Eve smiled. "I would—"

"Maybe a little later." Kenan slid his arm from around her and grasped her hand. "Eve promised me a dance first. We'll catch up with you, Gavin."

Tapping his fist to his brother's chest, he led Eve away from the bar and toward the crowded dance floor. Instead of pushing his way to the middle, he stopped on the edge and drew her close against him. Clasping her wrists, he wound her arms around his neck, then stroked his hands down to her shoulders, over the dip of her waist to rest on the flare of her hips. Her soft breasts were pressed to his chest, and as he slid a leg between her rounded, tight thighs, need, hungry and raw, clawed at him. It was impossible—his rational mind convinced him it definitely wasn't possible—but he swore the damp, feminine heat of her penetrated the layers of their clothes to sear him in the sweetest, dirtiest way.

"What are you doing?" Eve stiffened, leaning back to glare up at him. She shifted her hands from his nape to his chest, exerting pressure. "I may not be an expert in flirtation, but I can tell when a man is interested. And Gavin *was interested*. He asked us to join him, for God's sake. Why did you tell him no?"

"Don't push me away. Put your arms back around me."

Her immediate obedience triggered a primal response in him. A response that had him needing to praise her, touch her for that show of instinctive trust. In him. It stimulated his heart...and his dick.

He bowed his head over hers, and to anyone looking—to Gavin—he would appear to be on the verge of taking her mouth, a prelude to another kind of conquering.

"Lesson number two. A dog is man's best friend for a reason. Because we have a lot in common. For instance, a dog can ignore or play and be finished with a bone. But as soon as another dog comes sniffing around, suddenly that bone is the most desirable, delicious thing he's ever possessed, and he wants it with a single-minded focus that's scary."

"I don't know if I want to roll my eyes at the man-baby ridiculousness of that or deliver a stinging diatribe on the indignity of comparing women to bones," she drawled. Her nails scraped the nape of his neck, and he wrestled back a shiver at the whisper of pain under the wave of pleasure. "Personally, the way I'm leaning includes the words *junk* and *punch*."

He shook his head, giving her a small smile. "Please, sweetheart. Don't act like you haven't heard that before. I'm just giving you truth as it pertains to Gavin. He invited you to join him in that VIP room, and if I hadn't stepped in, you would've agreed so fast, there would be skid marks on that staircase right now."

Her lips parted to object, but when he arched an eyebrow, she narrowed her eyes on him.

And remained silent.

"That's right." He nodded. "He put forth the barest amount of effort, and you weren't going to require him to do more. Your mother's an elder in her church, and God knows you spent enough hours there growing up. What does Scripture say about a man who doesn't work?" He lowered his head until their foreheads nearly brushed. "He doesn't eat."

Her eyes briefly closed and a puff of sweet, vodka-and-cranberry-scented breath bathed his mouth. "I'm about ninety-eight-point-nine percent sure that's not how God intended that scripture to be used."

He chuckled, and yes, it was filthy even to his own ears. "The concept's the same. So here's what you're going to do. Dance with me. Flirt with me. Pretend you've forgotten Gavin even exists. And make him come for you. Fucking *earn you*, Eve."

She blinked. Stared at him. And he stared back,

maintaining that visual contact as if his heart wasn't slamming against his chest because he'd said too much. Allowed too much passion into his voice, more than what belonged to someone who was only a friend.

After a long moment, she turned around, lifted her arms...and undulated her body against him. Like a match to dry kindling, he ignited in flames. He moved with her, losing himself in the pounding rhythm of the music, as it echoed the wild beat in his blood, his cock. It spoke of need, of greed. And he gave in to it.

Burying his face in her curls, he was no longer Kenan, and she ceased being Eve. They became two people, strangers, meeting, flirting with their bodies, letting a heat that had nothing to do with the crush of people rise between them. He became a man indulging in foreplay with a woman.

With each roll of her hips, she stroked her ass over his cock, and dammit, he should have shifted away, inserted space between their bodies. He should have. But he didn't. He clenched his jaw, entrapping the growl that rumbled in the back of his throat, and danced with her. Let her feel the effect she had on him. He'd find a way to explain it away later. Not that she seemed to mind. Maybe she was as caught up in this pretense as he was, because she didn't whirl around and accuse him with those beautiful eyes or tear into him with that sometimes sharp tongue. No. Instead, Eve rubbed over him again...and again. Teasing him, arousing him, tempting him.

Jesus, she was pure, condensed temptation.

A thick, erotic haze enshrouded his mind, settled in

his limbs, weighing them down even as it buoyed him. This—her in his arms, inhaling her sweat-dampened cedarwood-and-roses scent, her small, thick body grinding against him—was his moment to let go.

And he did. He could give himself this. He *owed* himself this.

She spun around, wound her arms around his neck and pressed her breasts, hips and thighs to him. Her hooded gaze met his, and even in the dark, he glimpsed… God, the glint of desire there. For him? Yes, he convinced himself. *For him*. Desire wrapped its hot, sticky fingers around his throat and squeezed, cutting off all ability to think, to process his actions, to consider the consequences.

He slid a hand up her back and tunneled his fingers into her hair, cupping her head, tilting it. His breath punched out of his lungs, and his heart hurled itself against his rib cage. To get to her? To escape him and spare itself from this colossal mistake he was on the verge of making?

Didn't matter. Not when his dick was in full control at the moment.

He lowered his head, close enough that he tasted his error on her parted lips. Its flavor was regret and greed.

Fuck it.

He took her mouth.

Invaded it. Claimed it. Sexed it.

Eve stiffened, and her shock vibrated from her trembling frame right into his. He absorbed it, his arm around her waist, curling her into his body. A warning blared through the dense fog in his head, and he started to draw back. Kenan was not so far gone that he would force what wasn't willingly offered. But then, she softened, melted into him, her lips opening wider, granting him more access.

He groaned, closed his eyes. And fell.

Urgency and years of need didn't allow him to be gentle or tender. Didn't allow him to ease into this mating of mouths, or leisurely explore this territory that was both endearingly familiar and terrifyingly new.

Being denied this—being denied *her*—for so long stripped him of his famed charm, of his control. Ruled by lust, by a soul-deep yearning and the knowledge that this would be his one and only taste of her, he delved into her. Twisted his tongue around hers and sucked and licked. He demanded. Demanded that she give in return. That she devour him just as eagerly, as desperately as he feasted on her.

And she did.

God, did she.

Her nails bit into the skin on his neck as she tilted her head, met him thrust for thrust, chasing his tongue for more. She didn't need to pursue him for what he wanted, needed, to give her. What he would beg for her to take. He stroked inside her, harder, deeper. And when she tangled with him, he couldn't have stopped grinding his erection against her soft belly. Barely stifled the howling urge to hike her up in his arms, wind those legs around him and rock into that hot, soft place between her thighs. She emitted a whimper that echoed in his chest, his gut, his cock.

But it was her needy sound that snatched him back to the dance floor in his brother's club.

What the hell am I doing?

The question ricocheted off the walls of his skull. Jerking up his head, he broke off the kiss. He barely managed not to return for one last sample, but he licked his lips, savoring that last bit of her. Because it would have to sustain him.

"Kenan," Eve whispered, slowly lowering her arms, resting her palms on his chest. She stared up at him, eyes wide but still a little hazy, lips swollen and damp from their kiss.

Slowly, he untangled his fingers from her hair and released her waist, stepping back. Placing much-needed space between them. As if that would help. It hadn't in fifteen years.

"Is Gavin still standing at the bar watching us?" He clasped her hand in his and lifted it to his mouth, pausing just shy of brushing his lips over it. "Do we still have him as our captivated audience?"

The clouds in her gaze cleared, and her head jerked back in a slight flinch. She stared at him for a long, charged moment, then glanced over his shoulder.

"Yes, he's still there." She shifted her attention back to him, her bottom lip pulled between her teeth. "So that kiss… It was for Gavin's benefit?"

I don't give a fuck about Gavin. I've been hungry for the taste of you for over a decade. And now that I've had your addictive, delicious flavor on my tongue, you might have ruined me more than I already am.

The admission roared so loud in his head, he paused

before replying, balancing himself, afraid he might have actually voiced it. When she continued to look at him instead of gaping in horror, relief poured through him.

He could do this. Pretend.

It was all a part of the show. And between trying to be the perfect son for his parents and the platonic best friend for her, he'd become one hell of an actor.

"Of course," he lied, tugging her close and bending his head over hers. "Remember what I said about him wanting what he believes another man desires? If that doesn't get his ass in gear, nothing will. And the fact that he's still standing there instead of heading to the VIP section means he either wants, or is interested in wanting."

"Jesus, Kenan." She touched a finger to her still-damp bottom lip.

And, dammit, he wanted to replace those fingers with his tongue.

He took another step away from her, but her hand clutched in his prevented him from moving far.

"It's just a kiss, Eve. A tool to get the job done. You want Gavin, and I want you for my Bromberg's project. I'm only holding up my end of the bargain."

Dammit. He was trying too hard to render that "hot as fuck" melding of mouths into something inconsequential. But it needed to be said. To ensure she didn't guess his secret and to remind himself that she wasn't his. That she was here in this club for his brother, the one she truly desired. Her response to his kiss could be chalked up to shock, to playing the game. He was the liar here; she'd never pretended to want anyone but Gavin.

Better he remember that and avoid any fanciful, foolish thoughts of "what if." He'd always come in second place with his parents, with his career and with her love.

But at least they had their friendship.

No way in hell would he fuck that up.

"Let's go see if it worked. You ready?" He arched an eyebrow.

Her intense scrutiny didn't waver from his face, and it unnerved him. Worried him.

Finally, she glanced away, and he almost groaned with relief.

"Actually, I'm going to head to the bathroom. I'll be back."

"I'll go with you—"

"No." She shook her head. "I'm okay, and I need a minute."

She didn't wait for his agreement, but walked away, leaving him to stare after her. After a few moments, he pivoted and strode back to the bar, where Gavin still waited.

"Hey, Kenan. Everything okay?" his brother asked, his gaze flicking in the direction Eve disappeared.

Okay? Hell no. Everything was most definitely not *okay*.

But Kenan smiled, hoping the darkness of the club hid how forced it felt. "Yeah, Eve just had to use the restroom."

"Good, just checking." Gavin nodded, then slid his

hands into his pants pockets and leaned against the bar's edge. "It's not my business, so feel free to tell me to mind it, but—" he hiked his chin up "—I thought you and Eve were just friends."

"We are." He shrugged a shoulder and caught the bartender's eye. Only after he ordered a whiskey and felt the liquid burn as it slid over his tongue and down his throat did he continue answering his brother. "If you're referring to what you saw out there, that was nothing serious." And the lies kept coming. Right. It wasn't *nothing*. It was *everything*. "Eve and I are friends."

"If you're sure. It looked like…"

"I'm sure." He took another sip of his drink, his grip on the glass nearly threatening to shatter it. "Why are you asking?"

He knew damn well why Gavin was asking.

Gavin studied him, then shook his head, a smile quirking a corner of his mouth. "I just want to make sure I'm not stepping on any toes. She's…" Gavin blew out a breath. "Fuck, she's gorgeous. Why haven't I noticed before?"

Kenan knocked back the rest of the whiskey to prevent himself from answering that stupid-ass question.

"She's always been gorgeous," Kenan said, voice smooth, even. "But, no, you aren't stepping on any toes. Eve is single."

"You sure you don't mind?"

Bitterness tinged with sorrow bloomed in his chest. "It's Eve's decision, not mine. But, no, I'm good."

Gavin's smile broadened, and he clapped Kenan on the shoulder. "That's great. Thanks, Kenan."

"No problem."

Right. No problem.

Eve would finally have the man she'd wanted for years.

And with the success of this project, he would finally have the recognition of being more than the "other Rhodes son" or a Farrell Bastard.

It was all he needed.

Seven

Lesson plans turned in. Check.

Grades updated. Check.

Netflix pulled up and *Bridgerton* loaded and ready to play...for the sixth viewing. Check.

Eve smiled as the doorbell rang, and she hopped off the couch, snatching up several dollar bills off the coffee table.

Large meat-lover's pizza with extra cheese and onions. Check and check.

The last three weeks had been filled with work—both at school and with Intimate Curves—and social events. Lord, so many social events. Kenan was taking his end of their bargain seriously. If a gallery opening, fundraiser or dinner party was happening and Gavin would be in attendance, Kenan escorted her there. And, damn, Gavin had an active social calendar. If she didn't know better, she'd suspect Kenan of feverishly trying to throw her at his brother…as if he was attempting to pawn her off on him.

It was ridiculous; they'd been friends for over two decades. Yet, that knowledge didn't stop her feelings from smarting like alcohol splashed on a scraped knee.

Before, she would've just asked him about it. Just demanded to know what the hell was up. But that pesky *before*…

Before that night in the club.

Before that dance.

Before that kiss.

Nope. Not going to think about it. Her first free Friday in weeks, and she intended to stay home, relax and not spend another second dwelling on that…

A shiver rippled through her, and she sank her teeth into her bottom lip, unwilling to free the moan climbing up her throat. Again. Friday. No date. No pretending she hadn't buried her tongue in her best friend's mouth. And liked it.

Hell.

Grimacing, she hurried to her front door like robed Dementors floated at her heels. Huh. Maybe she should indulge in a Harry Potter binge instead of sexy historical-romance shenanigans…

She opened the door, the delivery person's tip in hand, ready to exchange it for the pizza she'd paid for online.

"Hi… Kenan." She stared at her best friend, gripping the doorknob. Flutters that she decided to attribute to shock quivered in her stomach. "What're you doing here?"

"Better question. Why didn't you ask who it was before answering the door?"

"Look, *Dad*," she drawled. "Not that it's your business, but I was expecting a pizza delivery."

"Dad." The corner of his mouth twitched. "Kinky."

Laughter tickled her throat, but she crossed her arms over her chest, blocking the doorway. "What're you doing here? I thought we didn't have anything scheduled for tonight?" Leaning forward, she pinned him with a glare. "And if you say that we do, I can't promise you won't end up in a montage of pictures on ID Discovery as I talk fondly about you from my jail cell."

He snorted. Cradling her hips in his big, elegant hands, he shifted her backward as he moved forward until they were both standing in her apartment. He closed the door behind him, then turned to lock it, and she used that opportunity to assure herself her skin wasn't tingling from that tender but firm clasp.

That night in the club, he'd gripped her like that—gently, but with more than a hint of dominance. Then, electricity had crackled inside her, currents of heat moving through her. She'd flowed with it, letting go and losing herself for the first time in so long, confident and secure in the knowledge that Kenan would catch her, protect her. Even as he was the one sending her flying.

Even as the hot, thick weight of his cock grinding against her behind had kept her grounded.

And there went those flutters again.

Followed by a flood of "what the fuck?"

Kenan was her friend. Her *best* friend. And aside from that brief teenage phase, she didn't associate him in the same sentence with heat, flutters and cock.

She didn't…right?

Right, dammit.

And, yes, she was negotiating with herself.

"At the risk of repeating myself for a third time…" She headed to the kitchen and the bottle of wine she'd bought on the way home to drink with her pizza. Classy. That was her. "But, seriously, what are you doing here?"

"Where else would I be?" He followed her and leaned a hip against the breakfast bar that separated the spacious living area from the kitchen.

"Let's see." She tapped a finger to her bottom lip, squinting at the ceiling. "Friday night. You're single. And you don't have to escort me anywhere. All that equals freedom." She smirked, opening the refrigerator and pulling out the wine. "So if you don't have to hang with me why are you here at my house?"

"First, let's make one thing clear. I've never had to hang with you. This might come as a surprise to you, given your often curmudgeonly demeanor, but I enjoy your company."

"Spell *curmudgeonly*," she muttered, then narrowed her gaze on him. "Isn't there a party you should be attending? Business associates to schmooze? Beautiful people to entertain?"

He studied her for a long moment, his bright gaze piercing but shuttered. "If I didn't know any better,

I'd think you were trying to get rid of me, Eve," he murmured.

Guilt shimmered inside of her. How did she explain that for the first time in their long friendship, she needed a break from him, from the stunning vitality of him? The nearly visceral sexuality of him.

It was startling. Disconcerting.

Confusing.

And she'd wanted time to find her equilibrium and figure out how to return to the easy familiarity they shared. One not threaded and *alive* with this awareness.

Awareness? Why don't you call it what it is?

Nope.

Damn. More arguing with herself. She really should've bought another bottle of wine.

"That's ridiculous." She dismissed his very accurate conclusion with a wave of her hand, then popped the cork free of the wine bottle with a corkscrew. Scooting her glass closer, she focused all her attention on pouring the merlot as if scrying the deep red alcohol for the answers to the universe. "I just would've thought you'd want a night off from me."

"Eve." He flattened his palm on the counter near her drink. "Look at me."

Slowly, she set down the bottle and lifted her gaze to his.

"Are you having second thoughts?" he murmured.

She froze, her hand hovering near the glass stem. Second thoughts? Was she?

Their plan appeared to be working. Gavin flirted

with her, not hiding his attraction or his desire to get closer to her. And she would be lying if she claimed not to be flattered by his attention. After craving it for so long, who wouldn't be thrilled? Gavin was handsome, smart, charming, successful...

And yet...

Her gaze dipped to Kenan's mouth. Yet, she couldn't exorcise that damn kiss from her mind. That wet, lush, raw tangling of lips, tongues and sighs that haunted her during the day and chased her into her dreams. It'd shocked her then, and now, how quickly she'd surrendered to that undertow of lust, letting it drag her under until she forgot all about clubs, people and thoughts of "what the hell am I doing?" That kiss had shamed the ones that had come before it and ruined the ones that would follow. Arousal slid through her like melted butter—warm, soft, utterly delicious...and so fucking bad for you.

But while her world had been rocked, apparently Kenan hadn't even suffered a 0.5 on the Richter scale. It shouldn't bother her; Kenan enjoyed a reputation as one of Boston's most eligible bachelors, a lovable but elusive playboy. He wasn't a stranger to kissing women. Still, maybe if she could erase from her head how she'd clung to him, whimpered into his mouth then walked away aching and wet while he stood there unmoved, maybe she could extinguish the humiliation in her belly.

Stop being silly. She shook her head, raising her glass for a deep, long sip. Of course, he'd been unaffected. Kenan had never exhibited any signs of desire for her, even as a teenager who probably got stiff with every passing breeze. She'd always been nothing but a friend to him.

Which was fine, because she wanted Gavin, not Kenan.

Are you su—

Oh, shut up.

Wine. Wine, wine, wine.

"No," she said, finally answering his question. "I'm not having second thoughts. Why would you think that?"

His blue-gray eyes roamed over her, and with liquid courage warming her veins, she met that intense scrutiny.

"Eve, I don't—"

The doorbell rang, and she swallowed her sigh of relief. "Pizza's here. Are you staying?"

"Have I ever turned down free pizza?" Before she could answer or head toward the front door, he held up a hand. "I got it. You want to get plates and pour me some of that wine? Especially since you're staring at that bottle like a lion about to chase down a gazelle."

Ass.

He wasn't wrong, though.

A few moments later, he returned with a large, grease-spotted pizza box, and the orgasmic scents of oregano, cheese and crisp dough stained the air. Her stomach growled, and Kenan, arching an eyebrow, didn't even have the grace to pretend he didn't catch it.

"Oh, shut up." She set plates and napkins on the coffee table. "Put it here, and I'll get the wine."

For the next forty minutes, they ate pizza, drank wine and watched the first episode of *Bridgerton*. That familiar, easy comfort they'd always shared returned, and by the time Simon and Daphne enacted their fake-relationship arrangement, she was glad Kenan had shown up at her door. She'd missed evenings like this with him.

"If Daphne hadn't taken the duke up on his offer, I would've," Kenan said with a shake of his head. "Simon is fine."

She snickered, then picked up the remains of their dinner and carried them into the kitchen. When she returned, Kenan had her sketch pad in his hands. That instinctive urge to snatch it away, flip the lid closed and hide away her drawings flared within her. She curled and straightened her fingers, reminding herself this was Kenan. Not a stranger. Or her mother.

Yolanda had never understood Eve's need to create, to lose herself in filling up page after page of her many sketch pads. Especially with things her mother had considered frivolous and useless, such as fashion. Eve had learned to be protective and secretive early, and some habits died a very slow death.

"You still draw in your pads first?" Kenan studied a page, and anticipation and nerves dueled it out inside her.

"Call me old-fashioned, but I initially like to get the vision out of my head on paper."

He finally lifted his gaze, and her breath jammed in her throat at the burning admiration that lit his eyes like a blue flame, nearly eclipsing the gray.

"You're so fucking gifted, Eve."

Pleasure suffused her. Kenan had never been stingy with compliments, but he'd really been the only one in her life who'd offered them to her. She'd never doubted her mother's pride in her or her love, but Yolanda wasn't an emotionally effusive person. Her mother exhibited love through her actions, such as providing for her, pushing her, motivating her. But Kenan, he'd given her the words, the praise, no matter how difficult a time she had accepting them.

"Thank you," she murmured. Clearing her throat, she approached the couch and removed her tablet from her laptop bag. "I'm not finished yet, but would you like to see a few of the designs I'm working on?"

Excitement brightened his eyes, reminding her of a child spying his gifts on Christmas morning.

"Absolutely."

She lowered to the couch, and he sank down next to her. His crisp and earthy scent teased her, and the heat from his thigh pressed alongside hers threatened to derail her concentration. Inhaling a low, deep breath, she tapped the tablet's screen, bringing up her program and the lingerie sketches she'd been working on.

"Here you go." She handed him the device and waited, stomach in knots.

This was the first time she'd designed pieces for another project other than her website and store. It didn't escape her that Kenan had hung the bulk of the success of his rebranding proposal on her designs. And she would do her very best to come through for him.

For the next several minutes, he studied the sketches,

scrolling through from screen to screen. Objectively, she could admit that she'd done some of her best work. But would the butter-yellow demi bra created in the shape of a butterfly, with the wings forming the lace cups, and the matching boy shorts fulfill his expectations? Or maybe the mesh-and-lace lilac bustier with the ribbon lace-up detail in the front and the high-cut panties in the same material? She loved both pieces, but that didn't mean he would see and understand her vision…

"When I first thought of this project and asked for your help, I had zero doubts you would come through for me." Kenan lifted his head, his bright gaze gleaming. "But, Jesus, Eve. You've exceeded what I hoped for and expected. Just when I think you can't surprise me…" He shook his head and his attention dipped back to the tablet. "These are fucking brilliant. Thank you."

Relief and delight fizzed and bubbled inside her like the most expensive champagne.

"You don't have to thank me." She waved her fingers. "It's not like I'm not getting exposure from this deal."

"No, I do have to thank you," he said, lowering the device to the coffee table.

For a moment, he trailed his fingertips over the screen and the black racerback with the rosebud appliqués and scalloped edges. When his gaze returned to hers, she fisted her hands at her sides. Either that or go to him, drag him down to the couch and hold him until that stark, almost haunted look disappeared from his eyes.

"Kenan," she whispered.

"You give me hope, do you know that?" he mur-mured, lifting his hand between them. It hovered over her cheek, but at the last moment, he lowered his arm and instead slid his hand into his pants pocket. "So many people believe you benefit from our friendship because of my last name and because your mother works for my father. But that's not the truth, is it?"

She didn't know how to answer that; she was one of the "many people." From the day he'd appeared in that break room, he'd become not just her friend but her protector, her comforter, her confidante. At times, her savior. So, no, she couldn't affirm his truth.

"When everyone else in my life doubted me, didn't see me as strong enough, smart enough or 'Rhodes' enough, you never did. You always accepted me, and I found a place to belong. You gave me that."

Sorrow, pain and love for him swirled inside her, a furious storm whipping at her, howling *for* him. She'd been a witness to his family dynamic for the past two decades. And it never ceased to infuriate her. Nathan Rhodes was a good man—a loyal husband, a dedicated father, a provider. And he'd never expressed that he fa-vored Gavin…but his actions had declared his prefer-ence. Every time Nathan praised Gavin for his grades but criticized Kenan's one B in the midst of all A's… When he attended all of Gavin's football and basketball games but only made a few of Kenan's… When he car-ried both sons to his office but only spent time tutor-ing his oldest on the inner workings of the company…

When Nathan claimed that he desired both sons

be enfolded in the family business, but trusted Gavin with the authority, titles and responsibility, he'd made it abundantly clear that his oldest received the lion's share of his respect, if not his love.

Eve resented Nathan for his constant dismissal of Kenan. And she couldn't understand how Dana could stand by and allow this treatment of the child she'd adopted and raised with the promise to love as much as her natural son.

Eve briefly closed her eyes, shoving down the anger. That wasn't what he needed from her right now.

"You gave me the same. And more, Kenan. You still do."

A dark emotion flashed through his gaze, but she didn't have time to decipher it before he bent his head and once more stared at the tablet with her designs.

"I feel useful at Farrell International in a way I never did at Rhodes Realty. I feel…wanted." He cleared his throat, then got off the couch, stepped back and picked up his glass of wine, taking a long sip. She didn't speak as he peered down into the ruby depths, but her palms itched to touch him, soothe him. "Cain welcomed me, trusted me with the company's marketing and PR. But this rebranding proposal? It's huge for me. This will prove to everyone that I deserve to be at Farrell. And not just because Barron fucked up and got a woman pregnant, leaving me with his DNA. It'll show that I earned my place there. Asking Cain for this opportunity was scary as hell. But as soon as you agreed to be on board, some of that fear disappeared. Because as long as I know that you have my back, I'm strong. I'm damn near indestructible."

God, what he did to her.

Break her. With his words, flashes of his unexpected vulnerability, he could just…break her.

Her feet moved before she gave them permission, and in just a few steps, she stood in front of him…then she wrapped him in her arms. She pressed against him, holding his tall, solid frame, relaying without words that she had him.

"You don't have to prove that you belong at Farrell. Or show anyone that you deserve to be there. There is no *deserving*. You are Barron's son as much as Cain. Being there is your right, and you bring your brilliance, your work ethic, your particular insight and talent to them. *They* should be thankful they have *you*. And just from the time I've spent around Cain and Achilles, they are. Those who can't see what you bring to the table, or refuse to acknowledge it for whatever reason, can go screw themselves."

He didn't reply, at least not vocally. But his arms tightened around her. But it wasn't enough. She needed him to confirm that he heard her. That he *believed* her.

She tipped back her head, but as her gaze met his, the gentle reprimand on her tongue died there. His blue-gray eyes burned as if lit with a flame, and the thought of being consumed by that bright fire flitted though her head.

He lifted a hand, and unlike before, this time he touched her. Brushed his fingertips over her jaw, her temple, her cheek. Her pulse drummed in a frantic, primal beat, and its throb echoed in her head and her throat, and between her legs. Anticipation. It dripped into her like an IV, straight into her veins. Anticipation and...want. Pure *want*.

Move.

Step away.

End this.

All wonderful, wise advice that her mind hurled at her. But she ignored it all. Because something had taken ahold of her—something achy, hot and wholly inappropriate for a best friend.

"Kenan," she whispered.

Again, no answer, but his fingertips ghosted over the curve of her bottom lip. Nerve endings she hadn't known existed lit up and danced in glee. On a shuddering breath, she closed her eyes, tilted her head—

The sudden, shrill ring of her cell pierced the room. *Funny*, she mused, flinching. It hadn't seemed jarring until this moment. Until she'd been about to quietly beg her friend for his mouth.

Thrusting her fingers in her hair, she whipped around, searching for her phone. Or she used that as a handy excuse. Her heart pounded against her rib cage, but for a different reason now. Jesus, what had she been about to do? What was she thinking?

You weren't. That's the problem.

She didn't see any point in arguing with herself this time. Not when she happened to be right. She would've kissed Kenan. Again. And this time, she wouldn't have the excuse of a pretense.

Spying the bottom half of her cell peeking out from

under a couch cushion, she skirted the coffee table—and Kenan—and dove for it. Without bothering to glance at the caller ID, she swiped at the screen and answered.

"Hello." Dammit. She sounded breathless even to her own ears.

"Hey, Eve. This is Gavin."

Shock doused her in a frigid wave. And right underneath lurked guilt. Unbidden, her gaze shifted to Kenan.

"Hi, Gavin. How're you?"

A random person would've missed the subtle change in him. But, knowing him as well as she did, she caught the tension that stiffened his powerful body. Noted the slight flattening of his sensual mouth. Noticed the taut skin over his cheekbones, causing the dusting of cinnamon freckles to stand out in stark relief.

"I'm fine. Better now that I have you on the phone." His blatant flattery should've had warmth cascading through her, but instead she struggled to even concentrate on the conversation. All of her attention was laser-focused on the silent, brooding man several feet away from her. "Are you busy?"

She glanced away from Kenan. No way in hell she could look at him and continue to talk to his brother. Not when she could still feel the promise of his kiss on her lips. Taste it on her tongue.

"No, not really. I'm just relaxing at home for the night."

"That sounds like a perfect evening. Especially if

I could spend it with you," Gavin said, his voice lowering, deepening.

Wisps of pleasure shivered inside her, and warmth flowed into her cheeks. She couldn't misread the flirtation in that statement. Flirtation, hell. Gavin Rhodes wanted to spend time with her. Part of her—the part that reverted back to a shy, crushing teenager—delighted in his words.

"I'm sure you have more exciting plans on a Friday night then spending it bingeing on Netflix," she murmured.

The nape of her neck prickled with awareness. She didn't need to peek over her shoulder to confirm that Kenan's stare would be pinned on her. It touched her. *Branded* her.

"You'd be surprised at how exciting that sounds." Gavin's chuckle resounded in her ear. "But, unfortunately, you're right about me having plans tonight that I can't get out of. Which is why I'm calling to see if I can claim your time for next Friday. I want to see you outside of a party or opening. I'd like to take you out, Eve."

"Oh, um…"

This was what she wanted, right? Gavin's interest. His attention. His desire. Years. She'd longed for all of this for years, and now, when she hovered on the verge of it being in her grasp, she hesitated.

She didn't bother asking herself why. The "why" stood behind her.

No. She pinched the bridge of her nose. Kenan didn't want her; other than that kiss, which he'd brushed off as part of their charade, he'd never given her any indication he felt the same inconvenient and inexplicable lust that had coursed through her just a few minutes ago. He'd always been affectionate, touching her, hugging her. It wasn't his fault that her hormones had decided to throw their panties at him.

God, this was wrong. On so many levels.

Kenan was her best friend. That's it. He had available women—plenty of them—who scratched his sexual itch. Who had permission to survey the landscape of his hard, perfect body. And she wasn't one of them. Would never be.

Which was fine because she wanted Gavin. He was her unobtainable fantasy that was suddenly very obtainable. Now wasn't the time to be distracted from that goal.

Exhaling a long, silent breath, she nodded, even though Gavin couldn't see the gesture. "Yes, I'd love to go out with you."

"Wonderful." His satisfaction and delight reached out to her. She should be enjoying this moment. But the knots twisting her stomach wouldn't permit it. "I'll call you next week with details."

"Sounds good."

"Eve…" He paused, and she closed her eyes, as if that could somehow fill the emptiness that yawned inside her. "I'm already counting down the days until Friday. I'll talk to you later."

She murmured a goodbye and ended the call. A deep silence filled the room, and its heavy, icy weight pressed down on her chest. She'd done it; she'd grabbed Gavin's attention. She was going on a date with him.

The elation, the effervescent happiness that came from victory, would fill her at any moment. Yes, any moment it would replace the edginess. Scrub away the cloying, grimy sense of betrayal.

Tossing the phone to the couch, she turned around and forced herself to meet Kenan's gaze. What had she expected? Anger? Irritation? Satisfaction, even?

Anything but a cold blankness that completely blocked her out of his thoughts.

Shock and hurt punched her in the gut. He'd never looked at her like that before.

He'd never shut her out.

"Congratulations," he murmured. "This is what you wanted."

Yes, it was…wasn't it?

Confusion swirled within her. She should be celebrating. And yet all she wanted was…what? To return to that easy camaraderie they'd shared for decades? To thank him for helping her obtain her dream man?

To cross the space that separated them and return to his arms? Beg him to ease the ache, satisfy this nagging need…?

"Thank you for dinner. I'm about to head out." He pivoted and strode for her front door, snatching up his coat and shrugging into it.

"Kenan," she called out, unsure what else to say, just that she couldn't let him leave. Didn't want him to leave. Not like this.

But he didn't stop, didn't turn around. Instead, he paused, his hand on the doorknob.

"Enjoy yourself, Eve," he said. "You deserve it."

She stood, frozen, as he let himself out of her apartment. And she continued to stare at that door long moments after he closed it behind him.

Enjoy herself, he'd said.

Right.

Now she just had to find a way to accomplish that while worrying if she'd lost her best friend.

Eight

"I can't imagine losing a parent so young." Gavin shook his head, then lifted his glass and sipped his Macallan. "That poor girl. What she must be going through. Teaching isn't an easy job. Not only are you educators, but confidantes and part-time counselors..." He trailed off, eyes narrowing as Eve wrinkled her nose. "What was that look for? Did I say something wrong?"

Eve huffed out a short laugh. "No, you didn't. I would just hold up on the sympathy for my student. Especially considering not two weeks after telling me she'd been absent for three days and missed her midterm exam because her father died, I met said very alive father at a basketball game. Now either he's Jesus and resurrected, or he never died in the first place."

Gavin's loud crack of laughter echoed in the elegant private dining room he'd reserved for their dinner date. He propped his arms on the table, leaning forward. His eyes gleamed, the light from the candles dancing in their pretty brown depths. "Are you serious? Tell me you're not serious and this freshman didn't actually fake her father's death."

Eve grinned. "Oh, but she did. Even went so far as to create a funeral program, print it out and bring it in as proof. The girl was good. Or scary. Needless to say, the parent-teacher conference we had was very interesting."

Still laughing, Gavin fell back in his chair and rubbed a hand over his jaw. "What was her endgame? And did she at least explain why she went through all that?"

"I have no idea how she expected to keep that big of a secret. From what I understand, the father is a pilot and travels a lot, so maybe she thought her mother would be the one coming up to the school." She shrugged. "But she's fifteen and probably didn't think that far ahead. And I guess she believed missing school to travel to New York and see BTS was well worth the possible fallout from figuratively offing her father."

"Kids."

Their gazes met, and after a beat of silence, they dissolved into chuckles. When the hilarity ebbed, they continued to smile at one another across the table.

She'd had fun. So much fun.

Who would've thought she could be so at ease in the presence of her long-time crush and speak without her words tripping all over each other like a drunken frat boy? The hideously expensive Brazilian steakhouse, with its sumptuous decor, had only increased her nerves when she'd first arrived. Being led to a private room where Gavin waited with a heart-stoppingly romantic setting of candles, roses and soft music only heightened her anxiety. What if she spilled the wine? What if the dolman sleeve of her off-the-shoulder dress dipped into the olive oil when she reached for the bread? What if she accidentally choked and couldn't talk?

But she shouldn't have worried. Charming, funny and kind, Gavin had put her at ease. With a beautiful restaurant, exquisite cuisine and a handsome, amazing gentleman for company, the evening had been beyond what she'd imagined. Utterly perfect.

And she couldn't wait to leave.

Regret and guilt clogged her throat, and even a sip of freshly brewed, delicious coffee couldn't dislodge them. All through the evening of wonderful conversation and laughter, she should've been focused on the man across from her. But her mind kept drifting to his brother. What was Kenan doing? *How* was he doing? Was he mad at her? Was that why he'd been avoiding her this week?

The questions trampled through her head, loudly, rudely and with not one damn care when or where they did it. Like now.

And if that wasn't the definition of fucked up—that her thoughts were preoccupied with one man while she dated another—then *Webster's* needed to update their latest edition.

About twenty minutes later, she rose from the table, Gavin behind her, holding out her chair. She smiled up at him even as she swallowed a sigh. Because as much as she wished—longed for—her heart to race, it just went about its business behind her rib cage. Just pumping blood as if this was any old, ordinary day.

She'd dreamed about a night like this, with Gavin staring down at her with *that* particular light in his eyes, since she'd been a girl. And now that it was happening, she couldn't revel in it. Because something was missing.

No, not a vague "something."

Desire. Need. That belly-twisting, aching hunger that had her desperate to climb him like a rope ladder in a long-ago gym class.

Not like when...

Stop. Nope. Not going there.

Picking up her purse, she stepped away from the table and turned up the wattage on her smile. And, yes, she was overcompensating.

"Thank you for a wonderful evening, Gavin. I really enjoyed myself."

"So did I." He settled a hand low on her back as they walked toward the door of the private room. Then he paused, cupping her elbow, and turned her to face him. Tipping back her head, she looked up and her nerves returned with a solid, air-stealing blow. "Eve, I don't think I've been very subtle about how attracted I am to you. I'm just sorry it took me so long to do anything about it."

Because it took a makeover, new clothes and another man kissing me to make you notice me.

She shut down the uncharitable thought, but the faintly bitter dregs of it remained.

"Tell me we can do this again." His voice thickened, and he gently cupped her jaw. "I want to see you again."

Kenan's advice to make him work for her, to not give in so easily, whispered through her head. But she didn't need to call his words to mind. Didn't need to pretend to play coy. Her hesitation was real.

"Like I said, I had a great time tonight. And spending time with a friend over a wonderful meal is never a hardship." She smiled, and though it felt tight on her lips, she held it there. "School and my other responsibilities have kept me pretty busy, but call me next week? We can work out the details then."

And the time would grant her a reprieve to figure out what the hell was going on with her. Why the thought of another date left her cold...and guilty.

"Friends?" he repeated softly, brushing a thumb over her cheek. "Okay, I'll accept that for now. But know I'm not content with leaving it there." He lowered his head and brushed his mouth over the spot his thumb had just caressed.

A little later, she waved at him as the valet held open the door for her to duck into her car. Only once she'd pulled out of the parking lot and melded into the busy Friday-night traffic did she release her breath on a heavy sigh.

When she stopped at a light, she reached for her cell, scrolled to her favorites list and tapped Kenan's name. The peal of the phone ringing filled the car's interior. After the fourth ring, the automated voice clicked on, requesting she leave a message, but she pressed the screen on her dashboard and ended the call.

"Dammit, Kenan."

Irritation flickered in her chest, and her grasp on her steering wheel tightened. She glanced at her dash again—9:17 p.m. In the three times she'd managed to catch him on the phone this week, he hadn't mentioned plans. But then again, he probably wouldn't have. But whether he was at home or out painting the town a particularly lascivious shade of red, he could *answer his damn phone*.

The irritation flared into anger, and she narrowed her eyes on the road. For some reason, he'd been punishing her since last Friday, and screw it, she was through letting it go. He was going to talk to her. Because that's what friends did. It seemed he'd forgotten that.

Well, fuck it.

She was going to remind him.

Kenan peered at his laptop's screen, but the art concepts the marketing team had sent over for him to approve could've been hieroglyphics for all he comprehended them. The longer he stared, the more the visuals blurred, the more the notes his team added became a muddled mess.

"Shit." He shoved back from the desk, his chair rolling over the hardwood floor. Rubbing his palms down his face, he muttered, "Shit," again, and dragged his hands over his head.

Sitting here trying to work when his concentration had ceased to exist hours ago was a fool's errand. And if he spun around and gazed out the dark bay window of his home office, he'd catch a reflection of that fool.

He stood, then rounded the desk and stalked to the built-in bar on the far wall. He should've taken up Cain and Devon on their offer to have dinner with them. Even going to that mausoleum Barron Farrell had once called home and had left for Cain would've been better than holing up in his too silent, empty Back Bay brownstone. Or, since he didn't live far from the Back Bay Fens and Fenway-Kenmore hugged the other side, he could've gone to any number of the restaurants and bars that were always busy on a Friday night.

Instead, he poured his third Glenlivet and brooded. Yes, he'd become *that* guy. The brooder.

Sipping his whiskey, he retraced his steps. But instead of settling back at his desk, he moved to the window. The moon illuminated the private, walled-in garden behind his brownstone, transforming it into a nocturnal, mysterious enclave of hedges, stone benches and a dormant fountain. Yet he could appreciate none of it. Saw none of it.

Not when images of Eve smiling and laughing with Gavin occupied his brain like a squatter. Visions of her turning up her gorgeous face to him, accepting his touch, his kiss. Would she go home with him after dinner? Let him take her to bed, caress that sexy body...?

Fuck.

He was torturing himself. Had been all evening. Hell, all week. He'd vacillated between reminding himself that this was their bargain and dialing her to demand she cancel dinner with his brother. That she was his, had always been his.

Lies.

He'd become accustomed to spinning them in his life, but he tried never to deceive himself as he remained the only person he could truly be honest with. And that truth hadn't changed in fifteen years. She wasn't and never would be his—not in the way his body needed. Not in the way his soul craved.

Bowing his head, he stared into the golden brown depths of his glass. Exhaling, he knocked back the rest of the alcohol. At least he had it as a companion to get through the night. A few more shots and he wouldn't even remember his own name. Oblivion sounded real sweet right about now.

"Since you're here, not comatose and seem to have all of your body parts, I'm going to assume you're fine and just ignoring my calls on purpose."

His heart slammed against his sternum, and his body tightened, adrenaline pumping through him. But then the voice and words registered, and his shock at suddenly not being alone in his house released him.

He slowly turned, lowering his empty glass to his desk. And met Eve's furious glare.

As the surprise retreated, the familiar dueling emotions of delight, lust, pain and love surged in. Even though the distance of the room separated them, he swore her fresh, cedarwood-and-roses scent teased him, had his mouth watering for a taste.

His gaze lowered, and he felt a spasm in his gut. The walnut-brown skin of her shoulders, bared by the dark red dress that flowed over her body before molding to her thick, tight legs, gleamed in his office's light.

She'd worn this for Gavin. Gone to him looking like living, breathing sex.

He picked up his glass and strode over to the bar. "Kenan."

"I gave you a key to my house for emergencies. Fire. Flood. My imminent death from a fall and crack on the head. Since neither flames nor water are destroying my crown molding, and I'm vertical, I'm assuming," he said, tossing her words back at her, "that this isn't a real emergency."

"Well, when you refuse to answer my calls and are suddenly too busy for even a lunch, I thought that fall scenario could've been possible and let myself in," she drawled.

Out of his peripheral vision, he watched her stride over to him. She snatched up the glass he'd just splashed alcohol into and threw it back. Reluctant admiration wavered inside him as she didn't even flinch from the strong hit of whiskey. She slammed down the tumbler on the bar top.

"Thirsty?" He arched an eyebrow.

"Pissed. I'm hoping the liquor will mellow me out

long enough to listen to your explanation for why you're avoiding me."

Kenan refilled his drink and raised it to his mouth for a long sip. Stalling. He could admit it. But could he confess that, yes, he'd cut her off this week? It'd been painful but necessary. He'd needed distance to get his head together, so when he finally saw her again, he could maintain the facade of being happy for her and Gavin.

He wasn't there yet.

Especially with her standing so close that her body heat warmed him. If he inhaled, would he catch his brother's scent mingling with hers?

He stepped back. Another step. And another.

Giving her his back, he walked to the dark fireplace and paused in front of it, staring at the framed pictures on the mantel. Him with his parents and brother. Him and Gavin. Him, Cain and Achilles in the garden behind Achilles's home. Him and Eve. Several of them through the years.

His friend. His secret. His heartache.

Jesus, if he could, he'd exorcise his feelings for her. Purge them so they could both be free. Briefly closing his eyes, he took another sip of Glenlivet. It'd ceased to burn after about drink two, but when the warmth hit his stomach, he savored it. Welcomed anything that beat back the ice in his bones.

"Kenan."

"How did your date go? Was my brother a perfect gentleman?"

Masochist streak still going strong, I see.

But as much as he hated himself for asking, he didn't rescind the question. He waited for her answer, a vise squeezing the hell out of his ribs.

Her heels clicked over the floor as she approached him. But she didn't stop next to him. Instead, she slipped between him and the fireplace, giving him no choice but to look at her. Look at the face that followed him into his dreams and offered him no mercy.

"Are you drunk?" She frowned.

He snorted and sipped from the whiskey. "Unfortunately, no." *Not yet.*

"Kenan, what's going on? Talk to me."

The anger bled from her expression, replaced by a concern that had the hairs on his arms and neck standing up. It veered too close to pity. And he hungered for a lot of things from her, but pity was not one of them.

It sparked a fury in him. Fury at himself for foolishly yearning for the impossible for so long. Fury at her for tormenting him with her scent, her voice, her damn *existence*. Fury at Gavin for always possessing what Kenan desired most—their parents' love, their parents' fucking DNA.

Eve.

Stretching his arms out on either side of her head, he deliberately set down his glass on the mantel and gripped the edge of it with both hands, caging Eve in. He shouldn't have delighted in the slight widening of her eyes. But he did. A dark, twisted delight coiled and tightened within him. And when he bent his elbows, leaning forward, he felt her swift intake of breath whisper over his dick in a filthy, sweet caress.

Goddamn, he'd offer up his soul on a lit pyre for the real thing.

"Talk to you?" he murmured, cocking his head, leisurely studying the delicate arch of her eyebrows, the coffee brown of her eyes, the impudent flare of her nose, the flagrant sensuality of her beautiful mouth, the gleaming teak of her skin… Hunger to touch, to sample, clawed at him. Coupled with the jealousy burning in his gut along with a good amount of alcohol, his usual control unraveled. "What should I talk about, Eve? How this week has been hell? Or how I've tried but can't evict you from my head? Or how the thought of you with my brother tonight has me seeking oblivion at the bottom of a bottle? Which topic do you want to tackle first?"

Silence crackled between them. The vestiges of restraint cautioned him to move back, grant her space. Find some way to joke off those charged questions.

He ignored them.

"Why?" she breathed, her gaze dark with surprise, confusion and…

That last emotion stirred a low, rough growl in his chest.

"Why, what? The hellish week, the eviction or the attempt to get drunk off my ass?"

"Yes," she breathed.

Another plunge into taut silence. Self-preservation clawed its way to the surface, and he shuffled a mental step back on the shaky limb he'd crawled out on.

"You first." He straightened, levering himself away

from her, although his arms still penned her in. "Why are you here instead of out with my brother?"

She blinked, and the tip of her tongue swept across her bottom lip. His fingers curled into the mantel behind her, and he locked his arms. His body damn near trembled with the control he exerted not to bend his head and retrace that damp path with his own tongue.

"The date's over. You didn't answer my call, and I was worried. So I came by to check on you."

Well, damn if that didn't cut deep. He didn't want her concern. He wanted—

Fuck.

This was pointless. He shifted his gaze from her to the whiskey on the mantel. He'd had enough alcohol for one night. Shoving away from her, he turned and headed toward the office door.

"Well, you can see for yourself that I'm fine. No need to worry." Scrubbing a hand down his face, he walked out into the hall and toward his bedroom. "Lock up behind yourself."

"Kenan." Her fingers wrapped around his arm, drawing him to a halt. Since he couldn't drag her with him, he stopped, but didn't turn around. "I lied." She circled him, coming to stand in front of him. Her throat worked as her lips parted, but no words emerged. Dropping her hand from his arm, she glanced away. "I…"

He didn't speak. Was frankly afraid to. Afraid of what would escape his mouth.

She skimmed her palms down the sides of her thighs, and his own hands tingled with the need to trace that same path.

"Yes, I was worried about you, but that isn't why I came by." She paused, gave a minute shake of her head, and a curl clung to her dark red-painted lips before she brushed it away. Hell. How ridiculous did it make him that he wanted to throw down with that strand of hair for the privilege it just enjoyed? "The truth... The truth is the date went great. Wonderful, even. Gavin was perfect, so was the food and conversation. But—" she lifted her gaze back to his, and his chest rose on a harsh, deep inhalation "—the entire time, I couldn't shake the feeling of it being...wrong. Because I couldn't stop thinking about you. You're my friend—my best friend, Kenan. I shouldn't have been sitting there regretting answering the phone last week. Shouldn't have been wondering what would've happened if I'd ignored it. Shouldn't have..." Her voice trailed off, but her fingers lifted, trembled just over her lips. "Shouldn't have been wanting your mouth on mine. Feeling it there. Needing it there again," she whispered.

Kenan briefly closed his eyes. Lust howled and snapped inside him, and only the most threadbare of bindings kept him in place. Prevented him from charging forward and crowding her against the nearest wall. Stopped him from hauling her in his arms and giving her his mouth and his cock.

At his continued silence, she staggered back a step. "I'm sorry." She pressed her fingertips to her forehead, dipping her chin. "Shit." Wincing, she edged around him. "I'm sorry," she repeated. "I shouldn't have— I crossed a line, and... Dammit, we're friends..."

"Eve." Heart a primal drum in his chest, he shifted,

blocking her path. Jesus, how could he speak, or fucking think, with so much need pumping through him? "Look at me."

"No, it's all right. I'm—"

"Don't make me beg." *That* had her gaze jerking up to his. He moved closer. And closer still until only a breath of space separated them. "Because I will. You have that much power over me." He bowed his head, whispered in her ear, "And I almost resent you for that."

Her soft, shaky gasp kissed his cheek, quivered over his dick.

"Kenan." Her fingers fumbled at his hips, then hooked into the waist of his pants, holding on to him.

"What, Eve?" He moved forward, ushering her backward until her back met the wall. Pressing his forearms on either side of her head, he surrounded her. And she besieged him—her scent, her warmth, the short, fast breaths on his skin. He was under her sensual assault, and fuck if he wasn't a willing prisoner of war. "Tell me what you want. Make it clear."

She didn't reply to his demand, but a hard shiver wracked her body, and it ricocheted through him even though the slimmest of spaces remained between them. He straightened his arms, levering back so he could peer down into her face. Glimpse the confusion and— *God*—desire that darkened her eyes to near black. Note her hesitation in the cinching of her eyebrows, the tightening of her lush mouth.

"You need me to say it?" he asked. When she tentatively nodded, he cupped her cheek then slid his hand into her curls, bunching the thick mass in his fist. "I can do that for you."

He surrendered to the driving urge to taste her. Just a little. He brushed his lips over her forehead. Over the bridge of her nose. At the corner of her mouth. He lifted his head, his pulse deafening in his head. Too far. He was pushing himself too far, too fast.

"You need me to take your mouth like I did in that club. Take it, bruise it, make you feel me long after the kiss is ended. But you don't want it to end, do you? You've been thinking about my hands on you." His voice deepened, roughened. Hunger twisted inside him, grabbing him, insisting he satiate it. "Wondering if I'd cup your breasts, mold them in my hands, or if I'd start with these pretty nipples." He dipped his head, taking in the hard tips clearly outlined beneath her dress. Beautiful. So damn beautiful and he needed them between his lips, on his tongue. He shook his head, raising his gaze back to hers. Jesus, what had he been saying? "You've been thinking about how I could give this petite, gorgeous body pleasure. How I'd push into you, filling you…" His mouth hovered just above hers, and he tasted each pant that painted her lips. "Fucking you."

She closed her eyes, that full, tempting mouth trembling.

That wouldn't do.

He craved the weight of that gaze on him.

"Eyes on me," he softly ordered. Once she complied, he cocked his head. "How did I do, Eve? Did I get it right?"

"Yes." Her grip on his waist tightened, pulled harder. "God, *yes*."

That moaned word splintered the last of his control.

He captured her mouth, plunging his tongue between her lips in a swift, carnal attack. They were past shy, gentle introductions. No, he consumed her like a lover who'd been here often. And he had.

In his dreams, he'd conquered her sweet mouth many times before.

He was a fucking connoisseur of her mouth.

Did Gavin kiss her? Is she coming to me with my brother on her?

The image of the two of them together, like this, tried to shove its way into his head, and for a moment, he stuttered, paused. Did he care? Yes. And no. If Gavin had tasted her, then he would wipe the memory from her. Brand himself on her. Tomorrow, her lips would still throb with his possession.

Sliding his other hand into her hair, he held her still and set about his mission. Corrupting. Marking. Owning. At least for tonight.

Eve tugged him against her even as she rose on her toes and met him stroke for stroke, lick for lick. Nip for nip. Their tongues, lips and teeth melded, clashed, battled. This wasn't a leisurely kiss, or a tender one. It was hurried, messy, wet.

It was perfection.

Goddamn, the fresh yet earthy flavor of her. He could gulp it down like his favorite Scotch and let it set him aflame. Drown him in heat and pleasure until he was completely intoxicated. He could become a glutton with her and regret nothing.

Which was why he should halt this now before they went too far and couldn't cross back over that line. He should—

"More." Her whimper slid over his skin in a silken caress. "Give me more."

He should grant her everything she asked—pleaded—for. It would be his pleasure…his honor.

With a groan, he possessed her mouth again and gave his hands free rein. First, her bared, graceful shoulders received his adoration. Then the strong yet delicate line of her collarbone. The slim, elegant column of her throat. He touched. He indulged. And with one last hard kiss, he lowered his head to follow the path his hands had tread.

Right there. Right in the hollow where shoulder and neck met. That cedarwood-and-roses scent greeted him, so rich and heady. He nuzzled the nook, licked it. Sucked it. Damn. Would this fragrance be thicker, even more potent, between her beautiful thighs? Oh, he intended to find out.

He dragged his lips over the top of her chest and slid his palms to just under her breasts. The weight of them rested on the back of his hands, and he stopped. Waited.

"Yes?" he asked, his voice little more than a hoarse rasp, sandpapered by lust.

Eve covered his hands with hers and pushed them up until he cupped her firm breasts, a shade less than a handful. They both groaned, and she arched into his hold, her head pressing into the wall. Her lashes fluttered down, her teeth sinking into her bottom lip. She was erotic art come to beautiful, carnal life.

Inhaling a breath that seemed infused with need, he stared down at his hands squeezing her, at his thumbs rubbing small circles around the taut peaks that pushed against her dress. Wonder sighed through him. He was touching her; this wasn't one of those nights when he woke up, sweating, hurting, with his cock in his fist. Because he could, he grazed his teeth over a dress-covered nipple, and satisfaction roared loud and fierce within him when she jerked, a small cry piercing the air.

Her hands flew to his head, holding him to her, encouraging him without words to give her what she'd demanded—more.

Reaching behind her, he located the zipper and tugged it down. Impatience rode him, and in moments, he had the dress stripped down over her hips and legs and pooled around her stilettoes.

"Fuck, sweetheart," he breathed, reverence heavy in his voice, his chest. Standing in front of him in a sexy strapless black bra, matching panties and heels, she stole the air from his lungs. And had hunger pouring through him like gasoline just waiting for the match. "You're beautiful." He brushed the side of her breast with the back of a knuckle. "So goddamn beautiful. More than I—"

He cut himself off, trapping the rest of that too-revealing sentence between his teeth. This was about tonight, the here and now. Tomorrow, she might very well look at him with regret in her eyes, and damn if he would compound the pain of that with a revelation of how he'd dreamed about her stripped bare and trembling before him. Because the tiny part of his mind not clouded with lust acknowledged that she would hurt him. There was no avoiding it.

But at this moment, while unsnapping her bra and filling his hands with her perfect breasts, the dark brown beaded nipples stabbing his palms, he didn't give a fuck. This—he dipped his head, sucked a tip into his mouth—was worth that inevitable pain.

She hissed, her nails scraping his scalp as she clutched him to her. And when he switched to the other, neglected breast, she guided him, lowering a hand to her flesh, holding herself up to his greedy lips and tongue.

By the time he sank to his knees, bracketing her hips in his palms and trailing his mouth down her stomach, she twisted in his grasp, working those rounded hips in a sensual dance that enticed him to join her. And he did.

With his mouth.

"Kenan." She choked out his name, rocking against him. "Please…"

He didn't need her to finish that plea; he understood. And he answered by nipping at her folds through the insubstantial lace of her panties. Hooking a finger in the soaked panel, he tugged the material to the side and feasted on her. He sucked and nibbled. But soon that wasn't enough, either. He removed her heels and yanked her underwear down and off. Then he returned to her, licking up that drenched path until he nudged the engorged bundle of nerves at the top of her sex.

Her muted scream punched the air just as her hips bucked forward. Growling against her, he restrained her restless, wild movements with an arm low across her belly, holding her still for his greedy mouth. With every lap and caress, every stroke and swirl over her swollen, hot flesh, lust gripped his dick, pounded in it, squeezed it.

He'd never come from giving oral sex before, but he'd never had his mouth on Eve before. And there was a first time for everything.

"Your choice, sweetheart." He tipped back his head, met her passion-glazed eyes. Pride and satisfaction blazed as fierce and bright in him as the need howling in his blood. No matter what happened after tonight, he'd put that flush in her cheeks, that haze of pleasure in her eyes. He'd sent shudders rippling through her, had cries breaking on her pretty lips. Him. "Come first on my tongue or on my cock." He licked a slow, teasing path around her clit, and her nails grazed over his scalp, trailed down to bite into his shoulders. "Tell me what you want."

"You." She gasped then moaned long and sweet as he slid two fingers inside her tight sex. "Oh, God. You."

He hummed, thrusting lazily, twisting his wrist at the end of each stroke. "Those weren't your choices. Mouth or cock, Eve."

For several seconds, she didn't answer, too consumed with riding his hand. And he allowed it, enraptured by the sight of her. She whimpered, bending over him to cup his face, slide her thumb into mouth. He nipped it, soothing away the sting with his tongue.

"You. Inside me," she rasped. "I need that. I need you."

He froze, those words penetrating the thick fog of lust to reach deeper inside him and fist his heart, brush his soul. Would he ever hear those words outside of this aberration of a moment?

Shoving aside the thought, he rose to his feet, fingers still pumping into her, still stroking her stiff nub of flesh. He crushed his mouth to hers, letting her taste herself on him. And she clung to him, driving her tongue between his lips, taking, taking...

"I want to give you gentle. You deserve it." He bent low enough to hike her into his arms. And when her strong legs wrapped around his waist and her hot, wet center ground against his abs, he didn't bother suppressing the rough sound of need that clawed its way up and out of his throat. "But I don't know if I can."

He'd wanted her too long. Even now, his body shook with that years-denied hunger.

"Don't be gentle. Don't handle me," she whispered against his neck.

Then she bit him. Lightly, but that soft sting arrowed straight to his dick, and he almost stumbled with her in his arms.

Steeling himself, he focused on stalking to his bedroom, entering and heading for the bed. Carefully, he laid her down on the mattress. And without removing his gaze from her gorgeous body of curves and dips and hollows, he removed his clothes in indecent haste. He'd become single-minded in his purpose.

Which was getting inside her.

He climbed on the bed, crawling over her body until he crouched over her.

"Kenan." She breathed his name, and the wonder that laced her tone as her gaze took in his bare shoulders, chest, thighs and his hard, erect dick. That visual caress had him throbbing, and he gripped himself, squeezing to try to alleviate that deep ache. He stroked himself, his fist sliding over his head, then sliding back down. Her lips parted and her heavy pants peppered the air. Pure hunger suffused her expression and his gut was hit with a spasm in response. She looked at him like she wanted to replace his hand with hers... or with her mouth.

Fuck. He might not survive this. But damn, if he didn't want to lay his life on the line to find out.

"You're stunning," she murmured, her scrutiny of him returning to his face. She cupped his cheek, levered up to brush a kiss over his mouth. Then dipped her tongue between his lips, tasting more of him. "God, you're stunning."

He buried his face in the crook of her neck, breathing her in. Hiding. Because he knew what his face would reveal.

A moment later, he shifted, reaching for the bedside dresser, and pulled open the drawer and removed a condom from it. Quickly, he opened the package and sheathed himself, then returned to her. Eve wound her arms around his shoulders, his neck, drawing him down to her. Damn, his heart. It thumped against his rib cage. Love, need and fear hurled through him at warp speed. Once he drove inside her, they couldn't go back. They couldn't undo this. Alarm sizzled down his spine, a warning.

"Is this what you want, Eve?" He threaded his fingers through her hair, gripping her head on both sides. "Be sure."

"I want this. I want *you*." Her hands slid under his arms and curled over his shoulders, tugging him close until his chest pressed against her full breasts. "Inside me, Kenan."

He closed his eyes and gave them both what they craved.

Heat. Pressure. Wet.

He locked down a hoarse shout as he pushed into her, but it echoed in his head. Nothing had ever felt this good, this *vital*. And nothing mattered but being completely surrounded by her. Embraced by her tight, quivering flesh. Everything in him hissed that he should thrust hard, sink inside her. But a small part of him that retained a semblance of sanity slowed, halted. Allowed her clenching sex to become accustomed to him. They were the best of friends; he knew it'd been a while for her. And though it stretched his control so far that sweat dotted his face, back and chest, he waited. Because possibly hurting her killed him more than being tortured by the sweet and sinful clasp of her body.

"This is about you," he whispered, nuzzling her jaw and scattering kisses along the delicate line. "Let me know when you're ready."

She slipped her hands down his damp back, over his hips, not stopping until she grasped his ass.

"Move. Please, move."

"Jesus, Eve." He groaned, slowly withdrew and released another moan when her flesh sucked at him, as if bemoaning his leaving. When only the head of his cock remained notched inside her, he paused, then thrust back home.

Home.

Because he'd never truly belonged, never really experienced a place of utter safety and beauty until this moment. Inside her.

He pulled free and plunged back into her again, slowly, tenderly. Gritting his teeth, he fought against the urge, the need, to ride her hard and raw. Despite what she'd said earlier, what he claimed about not being able to go gentle, he could give her this. Even if it drove him insane.

"You promised." Her harsh breath brushed his cheek, then his mouth, as she grazed her teeth over his bottom lip, then nipped it. "Take me like you need. Don't handle me."

As if her permission was the shears that snipped his control, he let go. Wrapping his arms around her, he cuddled her close and fucked her. Hard. Wild. Like he needed.

Like *they* needed.

Their bodies crashed together in a carnal war— loud, sweaty, laying siege to one another. With each short, fast thrust or slow, grinding glide, she gave it back to him in equal measure. Her cries and his grunts punctuated the air. The slap of damp skin greeting damp skin, the sound of her sex releasing and receiving him, created an erotic soundtrack that was now his favorite album. One he would replay over and over.

This couldn't last. Already that record skipped as electric pulses rippled up and down his spine, sizzling in the soles of his feet. Pleasure stretched him tight, and one wrong move, one sudden twitch, and he would hurl over that ledge into oblivion. But not without her.

Reaching between them, he swept his thumb over the stiff button of flesh, murmuring to her when she jerked and bucked against his touch. Once more. And once again. That's all it took for her flesh to clamp down on him in an almost brutal grip, milking him, coaxing his orgasm from him even as she shook and screamed in her own.

Somehow, he held back, riveted by the sight of her lost in ecstasy. He pistoned between her thighs, burying himself over and over, determined to wring every ounce of pleasure for her. And only when her whimpers echoed between them and her body started to go lax, did he unleash the fury spiraling inside him.

Part of him fought going over. He needed just a little more time inside her. Just a little. But his cock wasn't hearing it. Pleasure plowed into him, and he followed Eve into that abyss.

Afraid that when he crawled out, he would be alone. Again.

Nine

Kenan stepped off the elevator onto the fifteenth floor of the downtown office building. Silence greeted him, as did the familiar offices of Rhodes Realty. On a Saturday morning, no employees sat at the desks, the phones didn't ring and the hum of voices didn't fill the air. He would've thought it odd to be summoned to his family's business by his brother on a weekend if Kenan wasn't aware that five-day workweeks didn't apply to his brother or parents. When a deal called, they answered. Kenan had adopted the same work ethic. Although his father might not believe that Kenan had actually inherited something from him.

Exhaling a breath that seemed to echo in the empty offices, he scrubbed a hand over his head. Not only did he have to face his brother possessing the knowledge that Gavin wanted the woman Kenan had just been balls-deep inside, but now he also had to face his ghosts.

It'd been months since he'd visited this place that used to be his second home. Not because it contained painful memories. No, he didn't feel as if he would be welcomed. Not when he'd abandoned the company for Farrell. At least that's how his family defined it. Which only increased his curiosity over this mysterious request from Gavin. That curiosity hadn't been the only thing that had driven Kenan from his house, though.

Eve had.

Or, rather, thoughts of Eve. Because when he woke that morning after a night of the hottest sex he'd ever had, she'd disappeared. He'd reached for her again and touched cold, empty sheets. Any remnants of sleep had evaporated then, and in the hours since, he'd been vacillating between calling her and demanding to know why she'd crept out like a guilty thief, and avoiding his phone in case she did call. Hearing her voice and discovering she regretted the night before…

Yeah, ignorance was indeed bliss.

Giving his head a shake, he focused on his brother's closed office door. A vise tightened around his ribs as he glanced to his left and the door that once held his nameplate. It didn't any longer. That shouldn't have had pain spiking in her chest. But it did.

Hell, he'd been erased.

Clenching his jaw, he strode toward his brother's office. With a perfunctory knock, he opened the door.

"Hey, Gavin. What's all this—" He slammed to a

halt, noting the other two people sitting in the chairs in front of his brother's desk. "Mom. Dad." He frowned as Gavin straightened from his perch on the furniture. "This is…unexpected. What's going on? Is something wrong?"

"No, nothing's wrong." Gavin waved him inside. "Come on in."

Then why all the secrecy? Why do I feel like I'm being ambushed? The demands burned his tongue, but he doused them as his parents stood. Wariness sidled through him, but so did a cautious joy. He loved his family, and this strain on their relationship, this separation of the last eight months, had been a punishment. A punishment for a crime he hadn't committed.

Tucking aside that old wound with new scars for the moment, he closed the door behind him and walked farther into the office.

"Kenan." His mother held her hands out to him, and he grasped them, dutifully bending down so she could kiss his cheek. "It's good to see you."

He didn't miss the light note of censure in her voice. Translation: you've been too busy for your family.

"You, too," he murmured. "Dad, how're you?"

His father nodded. "Fine, Kenan."

So formal. So reserved.

In other words, business as usual.

"While I'm glad to spend time with you, I'm assuming there's a reason for this meeting. And that it's not just a coincidence that we're all here." He arched an eyebrow at his brother, who at least had the grace to look sheepish. "So what's going on?"

"Dad, Mom and I wanted to talk with you about something. A proposal, if you will."

Unease curled into a tight ball inside him, lodging between his ribs.

"Okay." His gaze shifted from his brother to his parents' matching stoic expressions, then moved back to Gavin. "I'm listening."

"For the last few weeks, we've been negotiating a possible project in Suffolk Downs with Darren and Shawn Young of The Brower Group for a mixed-use development," his father said. "The deal is almost closed."

"That's wonderful. Congratulations. A project with The Brower Group of that size means only good things for Rhodes Realty."

Nathan crossed his arms. "Exactly. I'm glad you understand that." He paused, and that unease in Kenan's chest expanded, sprouted roots that snaked down to his stomach. "Because Darren and Shawn have made it clear that they would prefer you to be a part of this deal. They like what you did with the marketing on the Allston Yards development last year and want you to replicate it for them."

Kenan frowned. "That's flattering. But they do know I'm not with the company any longer, right?"

His mother released a choked sound that could've been dismissive or signaled disgust. Probably somewhere in between, considering the topic. "Yes, they're very aware. Which is why they've issued this not-so-subtle condition as part of the deal. They want you involved."

Kenan's head jerked back. "Are you telling me that if I'm not included as part of the marketing team, then the deal doesn't happen?" What the hell was going on here?

Gavin stepped forward, sliding his hands into his pants pockets. "That's what was implied, but if push comes to shove, I don't know how serious they are about sticking to that stipulation." He glanced at his parents, his mouth firming before he shifted his attention to Kenan. "What Mom and Dad are trying to say—what *we* are trying to say—is that we'd like you to return to Rhodes Realty."

Kenan stared at his brother, any icy fist plowing into him. The cold crept inward to his veins, to his bones, until he couldn't move. A maelstrom of emotions swamped him. Yes, shock, but also anger because after all these months, they only wanted him back in the company when it might potentially cost them. Delight because, God, they needed him—his family wanted him. And pain because he was going to disappoint them; he had no choice.

"You know I'd love to help you in any way I could—" he held his hands out, palms up "—but I can't leave Farrell right now. I explained the stipulation of the will to you. For one year, I have to stay with the company or we lose everything—not just me, but Cain and Achilles, too. I've made a commitment, and I can't renege on that."

"So you would just let our company, our family company, suffer because you've defected to another business? For men you've known a matter of months, while you've been a part of us for thirty years?" his mother snapped. She laughed, but it contained no humor, only a scalpel sharp edge. "Does what we've built together mean so little to you now?"

What they'd built together? Bitterness coated his tongue. He'd never felt as if he truly belonged here. Only his last name had afforded him an office, because it damn sure hadn't given him respect. That had been offered unconditionally to Gavin, not him. Not even Kenan's talent as a businessman had been appreciated or acknowledged, especially not by Nathan.

But he swallowed down those bitter words. Dana didn't want to hear it, and Kenan recognized the futility of trying to make them understand. Frustration surged hot and bright, mating with a helpless anger that, for a brief moment, stole his power. Left him standing there as the boy who always felt like the orphan with grubby fingers staring into a window at the happy, *complete* family that he'd never be a part of.

Inhaling a deliberate breath, he shut down his feelings, boarded up his heart with a No Trespassing sign. If he didn't allow them entrance, they couldn't hurt him.

At least that was his theory.

"I don't believe I have to dignify that question with a response, because you already know the answer," Kenan quietly said. "You know I love you and would help you if I could. But you're asking me to break my word. And you and Dad have always taught me that a man's word is his bond. And if I go back on mine, it doesn't affect just me or Cain and Achilles. It harms employees, investors and countless others. I won't do that."

"What about a commitment to us?" his father demanded, voice as hard and unflinching as stone. It matched the gaze that narrowed on Kenan. "You made promises to us first that come with being family. None should take precedence over that."

"They're family, too, Dad," Kenan murmured. "As much as you hate to recognize them or their existence, they're my brothers."

"This is *bullshit*," his mother hissed, slashing a hand through the air. "Utter bullshit!"

Silence, quivering with shock and tension, descended on the office. Gavin and Kenan stared at Dana, stunned into speechlessness. Kenan could count on one hand the number of times he'd heard his mother curse, and he might have a couple of fingers left over. And while he'd witnessed her anger, she'd never trembled with it, red streaking her cheekbones. At her sides, her fingers curled and straightened.

Kenan glanced at his father, who studied his wife, his expression inscrutable.

"Mom," Gavin said, moving toward her. "It's okay. I—"

"No, Gavin, it's not. There's nothing about this that's *okay*," she snarled, then whipped around to Kenan. "*We're* your family, Kenan. We've been there for you all your life, and *we* deserve your undivided loyalty. Somehow, you've forgotten that, and I'm ashamed of you for it."

He flinched, a hole ripping open in his chest.

"For the last few months, you've lorded Barron Farrell over our heads as if he's some great savior because he gave you a company to run. As if that makes you better than us."

"That's not true," he murmured thickly.

But she didn't seem to hear him, she was so caught up in a vitriolic diatribe, one that she must've been holding in for a while. She stabbed a finger toward him, and continued, voice shaking with her fury.

"Well, let me enlighten you, Kenan. Regardless of his money, status and influence, Barron Farrell was a bastard, and you shouldn't be proud to claim him as your father or his sons as your brothers. There's nothing honorable in that last name. We raised you, loved you. But you're so caught up in their spell, you've forgotten that. Forgotten us."

With one last, long glare, she stalked out of the office.

Pain pulsed through him, pumped with each heartbeat. It stole his breath, his voice. How was he standing when every bit of him *hurt*?

"Kenan." Gavin took a step toward him, arm outstretched. Sadness weighed down his brown gaze. "She didn't mean that…"

Kenan looked at his father. "Didn't she?" he murmured, replying to his brother but maintaining visual contact with—issuing that demand to—his father.

Not waiting for an answer, he turned and left the office the same way he'd entered.

Alone.

Ten

Eve laid down her stylus pen, stared at her tablet and slowly smiled.

Oh, yes, she'd knocked this out the park.

Rising from the couch, she stretched, but her gaze remained on the screen with her latest design for Kenan's proposal. A complex but sexy crisscross of straps comprised the black bra-and-panty set, offering a peek-aboo of skin while also providing adequate coverage. The design was a flat-out tease, and she adored it. Kenan would, too…

She frowned, slowly lowering her arms.

Kenan.

It'd been a little over twelve hours since she'd sneaked out of his bed as if performing a walk of shame. In hindsight, she should've just woken him up and told him she was leaving. Or…

She could've stayed.

Closing her eyes, she pinched the bridge of her nose. Regret swarmed inside her, stinging. Not remorse over having sex with Kenan. God, how could a person bemoan multiple, reality-bending orgasms? She was no hypocrite.

No, she regretted the aftermath. Her uncertainty. The silence. The worry that they'd blown up a decades-long friendship.

The confusion, because God help her, but she didn't think she cared…

Groaning, she bowed her head, more than a little disgusted with herself. Had Kenan mesmerized her with his dick? That had to be the only explanation for why she was willing to risk their long relationship to have more of what he'd given her last night.

She was officially dick-matized.

She huffed out a ragged chuckle.

She was in so much trouble.

Even now, as memories from the night before filled her head, heat licked at her and she shifted, squeezing her thighs together at the ache tightening her nipples and blooming between her thighs. Kenan possessing her mouth like she was oxygen and he'd been deprived for years. Kenan kneeling before her, head tipped back, bright eyes burning up at her, lips swollen and damp with her. Kenan crouched over her, hard, beautiful cock notched in her sex, ready to push into her…

A breath shuddered out of her. That ache intensified

and she pressed a hand low to her belly. She wanted more—more pleasure, more orgasms, more of *him*. She was honest enough with herself to admit that. But the consequences of that "more" scared her. Her body might be willing to risk her friendship with Kenan, but her heart? Her mind? They weren't on board. Yet, with Kenan's silence all day, the damage might have already been done.

The doorbell rang, dragging her from the morose road her thoughts had traveled.

Thank God.

Striding to the door, her pulse sped. And, grimacing, she hated herself a little for it. She'd gotten over her preteen crush on Kenan eons ago. Reverting to that time of sweaty palms and eternal blushing didn't appeal to her.

Oh, oops. Too late.

Dammit.

Running her hand over her bound curls, she peeked through the peephole. Astonishment rippled through her, and she quickly twisted the lock and pulled open her front door.

"Hey, Mom. This is a surprise."

Yolanda Burke smiled at her, leaning in to kiss Eve's cheek.

"A good one, I hope. I haven't talked to you in a couple of days." Her mother moved forward, and Eve shifted backward, allowing her entrance. "I was out having dinner with some friends and decided to stop by and see how you were doing."

"You're right, then." Eve returned her mother's

smile. "This is a good surprise. Would you like something to drink? Coffee? Water? I was about to grab a glass of wine."

"I already had two glasses at dinner." Yolanda laughed. "I think I better take you up on that coffee."

"Look at you being a lush out in public." Eve grinned at her mother's snort.

She headed into the kitchen to prepare the coffee and her wine.

"What've you been up to? Work's been keeping you busy?" Yolanda asked a couple of moments later.

"Definitely. And it's starting to get warmer, so you know what that means." She chuckled, pouring the wine as the coffee maker brewed behind her. "Spring-itis. I'm fighting to keep their attention from the window, the girl or boy next to them, their phones. Everything but the lesson."

When her mother didn't answer, Eve frowned but continued preparing their drinks. Grabbing the coffee cup and her wineglass, she exited the kitchen and entered her living room. And drew up short.

Yolanda was standing in front of the couch, Eve's tablet in her hands.

The tablet that held Eve's latest designs for Intimate Curves.

Fear flooded her, filling her mouth until she almost choked on its briny taste. Her grip on the cup and glass tightened. She parted her lips to say…what? *Put that down. It's nothing. I've just been sketching again. It's not what you think.*

How about the truth?

She shook her head at that last suggestion. Keeping her secret from her mother had become such a habit that revealing it now wasn't even an option.

"What's this, Eve?" Yolanda finally lifted her head, flipping over the tablet and holding it up. As if Eve wouldn't recognize the sexy lingerie design. "Did you do this?"

Hypersensitive to her mother, she listened, ears straining, for any disappointment, any anger...or disgust. But she didn't catch anything. Nothing colored her voice. No, that wasn't true, either. Maybe curiosity? But how could that be true?

Eve was perched at a crossroads.

Continue to conceal the truth about her lingerie company from her mother and not risk upsetting and failing her.

Or finally confess and trust that their relationship would survive Eve's fear of not being the daughter Yolanda wanted...and, frankly, deserved.

Oh, God, she was scared.

Swallowing hard, she silently weighed her options over the symphony of her pounding heart. Fingers growing numb around the drinks in her hands, she forced her feet forward, fully entered the living room and set the cup and glass down on the table. Then she gently took the tablet from her mother and stared down at the design she'd been so proud of only minutes ago.

Scratch that. That she was still damn proud of.

And that thought made her decide which road to take.

"Yes," Eve said. "I designed this. It's one of many I've done."

Whew. Funny, she'd expected a weight to have lifted off her chest with that admission, but it still pressed on her rib cage. And when her mother tilted her head, pinning her with that unwavering gaze she'd employed since Eve's childhood, it became a little more difficult for her to breathe.

"One of many," Yolanda repeated. "I didn't know you were still drawing. I thought you'd stopped doing that in high school."

Here. This could be her out. Claim that, yes, this was just a hobby. But she was so tired of hiding this part of herself from one of the most important people in her life. So she inhaled and leaped.

"No, Mom, I never stopped. I couldn't if I wanted to, and believe me, I tried all those years ago. But sketching, art, designing—I love it too much." She paused, fear bottoming out her stomach, but she pushed on. "I adore teaching and it's been a great career. But... But it's not my only career. For the past four years I've run Intimate Curves, an online lingerie company catering to plus-size women. I own it and am the designer. This—" she tapped the tablet's screen "—is one of the designs that will be featured in my first brick-and-mortar store in the Bromberg's renovation."

Her mother stared at her, brown eyes almost black with shock. After several moments, Yolanda turned her head to the side, as if she couldn't stand the sight of Eve. That pit in Eve's stomach filled with pain, grief and anger. Was the thought of her designing underwear so salacious that her mother couldn't even look at her? Just because Eve didn't walk the path Yolanda believed she should, had Eve so horribly disappointed her?

I'm a successful businesswoman of an award-winning company. I earn a living doing what I love most. My business will be in a nationally recognized chain of department stores. You should be proud of me.

The rant reverberated in her head, and she strangled the tablet, her fingers aching in protest.

"Mom—" she rasped.

"For four years you've had a whole part of your life that you've kept hidden from me?" her mother interrupted, facing her again. Her eyes, which had been dark before, nearly smoldered with heat now. They narrowed on Eve even as her chin jerked high. "I'm your mother and until this moment I believed we were close, that we had the kind of relationship where you could tell me anything, but obviously I was wrong."

Wait. *What?* She was angry because she hadn't told her about the business? "Mom, I didn't think—"

"That's right. You didn't. Not about how it would feel to find out *years later* that my daughter thinks so little of me, of our relationship, that she would hide something as important to her as a business, a career. And for what? What have I done to you, Eve, that you would hurt me like this?"

Voice cracking on "this," her mother rushed around the table and toward the front door.

Panic attacked Eve and she charged after Yolanda.

"Mom, I'm sorry," she whispered. "I didn't mean to hurt you. This is on me."

"You're right this is on you." Yolanda grabbed the doorknob and yanked it open, then paused in the doorway. Her shoulders straightened even though Eve caught the catch in her mother's breath. "We're going to talk about this, Eve. But I need space. I'll call you."

She stepped outside and quietly pulled the door closed behind her. Eve stared at it and part of her wished that her mother had slammed it shut. That soft snick somehow seemed more accusatory, more condemning.

More final.

What had she done?

Minutes, or what seemed like hours or, God, *days* later, the doorbell rang while she was still standing there, and Eve lunged for the knob, twisting it and yanking the door open, her heart lodged in her throat.

Please, let me just have the chance to apologize. I'm so sorry. I swear, I didn't know—

"Kenan." She blinked, trying to adjust to seeing her friend on her welcome mat instead of her mother. "What are you doing here?"

"I came by to see you." He cocked his head, and his blue-gray gaze seemed brighter in her small, shadowed porch as he studied her with an intensity that she longed to hide from. "What's wrong?"

"What? Nothing." The automatic denial leaped from her, and she waved a hand. "Nothing," she repeated.

"Right." He stepped forward, and by habit, her feet moved backward, letting him inside her ground-level apartment. "And nothing is why you're standing there looking shell-shocked."

He closed the door behind him, locking it. Then pulled her into his arms. And the familiarity of his embrace, of his scent, of *him*, enveloped her, and the ice that had encased her since her mother left cracked. And she did, too, right down the middle.

Standing there in the foyer, she told him about her mother's visit and the resulting blowup. He listened, his hold on her never faltering even as her voice thickened with the admission that she'd hurt her mother and potentially damaged their relationship.

"I'm sorry, sweetheart," he murmured, his big hands rubbing up and down her spine. She burrowed closer into his tall, powerful frame, seeking his strength, leaning into it. "I know how much you love her and the courage it took for you to tell her the truth. I hate it for both of you that the conversation ended that way."

"You should've seen her face, Kenan." An image of her mother's expression flashed on the back of her eyelids and Eve flinched. "I've always been so afraid of disappointing her. That's what I was hoping to avoid by not telling her about Intimate Curves. And it's what I ended up doing, anyway. She might have been angry, but underneath, she was so hurt. I did that to her."

She eased out of his embrace and scrubbed both hands down her face. Pacing away from him, she let loose a small, humorless chuckle.

"All my life I've tried to be the perfect daughter for her. To compensate for being a burden—for being the replica of a man who didn't have the guts or the integrity to stick around. Can you imagine how painful it is to have a constant reminder of the man who abandoned you? So to make up for that, I've tried to never cause her worry or trouble or pain. Even if that meant giving up certain activities she didn't approve of. Even if it meant obtaining a degree and job in a field that didn't fulfill me, but it made her proud. It meant she didn't have to worry about me. She deserves that peace, that security. If the price was hiding a part of myself, then it was a small cost and one I was willing to pay. For her, I would do anything."

"But, sweetheart, did she ever ask you to?"

She paused midstride, whirling around to face him. "She didn't have to." She thrust out her hands, palms up. "Don't you see? She sacrificed for me all those years—it's my privilege to do the same for her. It's not something people who love each other should have to ask for."

Kenan slowly approached her as one might with an injured animal. And as offensive as that thought struck her, the sentiment wasn't that far off. The ache in her chest throbbed like an open wound.

"Eve." He swept a hand over her hair, his fingers curling into the bun on top of her head before continuing down, where he cupped the back of her neck. "We've been friends for a long time, and that affords me some leeway that others don't have, to be honest."

He lifted his other hand to her cheek and skated his thumb over her it. For a long moment, he peered down at her, those startlingly beautiful eyes too knowing.

"You are not, nor have you ever been, a burden. And it pisses me off to hear you refer to yourself like that. Almost as long as we've been in each other's lives,

I've seen you try to reach this unobtainable standard and expectation of perfection that no one set—not your mother, not an absentee father—except you. You have been too damn hard on yourself, have driven yourself... have punished yourself. And for what reason? For being born to a single mother? Hell, Eve, you didn't ask to be here. That was your parents' decision, your mother's choice, not yours. And I can say with an absolute certainty that she's never regretted her choice. She loves you. Would do anything for you. *Has* done everything for you. And I think you underestimate that love she has for you and yours for her when you deny your dreams and passion. She wouldn't want you to sacrifice either for her like some penance. That's an insult to her. To both of you."

He pressed his lips to her forehead, and Eve closed her eyes, savoring that caress as much as she soaked up his words. She didn't know if she believed them, but dammit, she grasped hold of them like a lifeline. Because, God, she wanted to believe him. She was desperate to believe him.

"You are a gift to her, Eve. And to me, too. And gifts are given without strings or expectations."

He was going to break her. Without even trying, he was going to break her open, and all the need, confusion and snarled feelings of fear and love were going to spill out all over both of them. And she couldn't have that. Not now. Not when she was so raw and uncertain about where they stood in this no-man's-land between friendship and...other.

Nodding, she stepped back, forcing his hands to

drop away. Good. She could think clearer when those big, mind-muddling hands weren't touching her.

"Your turn." She strode into the living room, making a beeline for her neglected wineglass. She needed it more than ever now. "What're you doing here? And don't try to tell me you were in the neighborhood because Back Bay is twenty minutes away."

With the question out there, a dense tension, fraught with sex, filled the room. At least on her part. Because images from the night before bombarded her—the two of them twisted, tangled and naked.

Snatching up her glass, she downed half in several gulps before turning to look at him. And from the gleam brightening that gaze until it damn near glowed, she guessed his thoughts had ventured in the same direction. But then he shook his head, glancing away. When he returned his scrutiny to her several moments later, that heat was banked, and frustration and disappointment comingled inside her.

Fine. They were going to ignore the topic of cataclysmic sex. Duly noted.

"Honestly, I don't know." He lifted a shoulder, a wry smile quirking the corners of his mouth. "I was sitting at home and had no plans for the evening, but then I'm in my car and sitting outside your house. I think I couldn't stand my own company."

"I understand that. I haven't been able to stand your company before." She smiled around the rim of her glass, taking another sip as he snorted. "There's something you're not telling me. Might as well spill, because if you drove all the way over here, I'm not letting it go."

When he didn't immediately reply, she exhaled. "Oh, shit. Is this going to require more wine?"

"Probably. Definitely. If you have anything harder, get it."

Minutes later, she had another bottle of merlot on the coffee table and passed him a glass filled to the brim.

"Sorry. Nothing stronger. Now tell me. Let me make it better."

He stared at her, and her breath caught at the flash of desire in his gaze. Yeah, her word choice could've been different. Damn if she'd take it back, though. If he needed her body again she'd willingly give it to him.

Lowering his thick fringe of lashes, he accepted the glass, their fingertips grazing and sending an electrified current snapping up her arm and tingling in her breasts. Silently, she ordered her nipples not to harden beneath her thin hoodie.

"It seems today is the day for family issues." He gave a low laugh that had her stomach tightening... and not in a good way. "Gavin called me this morning and asked me to come down to the office. When I arrived, my parents were there, too."

She frowned. "He didn't say anything about them being there? That's weird." And shady.

"No, and I soon found out why. They have a deal on the table, and one of the conditions of it is my participation as head of marketing. They want me to leave Farrell and return to Rhodes Realty." His lips twisted into a dark caricature of a smile. "Of course, Gavin had to say that part—my parents couldn't. Or wouldn't."

"Are you serious?" She set down her wineglass on

the table and leaned forward. "They just want you to quit a company you're part owner of and return to the fold. Just like that?"

He huffed out another of those humorless chuckles that pained her to hear.

"Just like that. Although, that's not how they view it. According to my parents, my loyalty belongs with them, not Farrell, or Cain and Achilles. There shouldn't be a choice. I believe my mother's words were they 'deserved my undivided loyalty and she's ashamed of me for forgetting it.'"

He delivered that news with a flippancy that didn't match up with the shadows swirling in his eyes or the death grip on his glass. Fury blasted through Eve, incinerating all thoughts but marching over to the Rhodeses's Back Bay brownstone and laying into their self-righteous asses for daring to question the fidelity and adoration of this son who'd always been so desperate for their acceptance and affirmation. Screw. Them.

But her anger wasn't what Kenan needed from her at this moment; he needed his best friend's listening ear.

"You know that's bullshit, right?"

He snorted. "That's exactly what my mother said when I told her I couldn't return to the company." Sighing, he set his glass on the coffee table next to hers and rubbed a hand over his mouth and chin, the scrape of his thick five-o'clock shadow against his palm a rasp in the room. "I haven't been able to escape that conversation all day. Thinking maybe they're right. I've known Cain and Achilles for months. *Months*. And my parents, Gavin—they're my family. If they need me, I owe them my allegiance."

"Okay, wasn't it you who just talked to me about not owing our parents? I called bullshit before, and I'm still calling it." She jabbed a finger toward him. "Let's just put aside the whole loyalty thing for a moment. Because time doesn't determine love or affection. Yes, you've known Cain and Achilles for a few months, but you've bonded with them. The three of you didn't come to know each other and work together under ordinary circumstances, and what you've been through since the reading of that will would unite anyone fast. But that's neither here nor there, because that's not the only thing at issue here, is it?"

She didn't wait for him to reply, but reached for his hand, taking it in hers. Stroking her thumb over the back of his knuckles, she met his unwavering gaze. She knew this man better than herself, and she ached for him.

"This is about making your own way. Standing on your own, apart from Rhodes Realty, from your family, and being your own person, forging your own path. Not as Nathan Rhodes's son or Gavin Rhodes's brother. Right or wrong, whether I agree with your reasoning or not, this is about you proving to yourself that you can make it on your own. And here's another thing to consider. You're happy at Farrell. Working with your brothers, who appreciate you, who listen to you. Do I believe you're putting undue pressure on yourself? Putting those same expectations and standards on yourself that you lectured me about? Yes. But you're challenged at Farrell, and you enjoy it. Why would you walk away from that? This idea of owing unconditional loyalty is your parents' hang-up, not yours. Loyalty is *not* unconditional. It's not blind. That's a fucking myth. It's earned. And while they have yours as the people who raised you, you don't owe them your life."

His gaze dipped from hers to their clasped hands, and he flipped his over so his fingers wrapped around hers and squeezed.

"We're a pair. Each giving advice but finding it difficult to take." A ghost of a smile flirted with his full lips. "Thank you, Eve."

"You don't believe me, though, do you?"

His stare lifted to meet hers. "Did you believe me?"

"Yes."

"Liar."

She narrowed her eyes on him, then shook her head and laughed softly. "Fine. I swear, I'm going to try, though." Pausing, she sobered and studied him, emotion that had too many names to parse lodged in her throat. "If you don't accept anything else, Kenan, receive this. You're the best man I know. Brilliant, generous, kind and, yes, loyal. You said I'm a gift to you? I'm the one who's been blessed to have you as my friend."

He lifted their hands and brushed his lips across her knuckles. There was a spasm inside her belly so hard, her breath caught, and she clenched her teeth around a soft whimper. Just this light touch already had her damp and pulsing with need.

"There's another reason I came over here," he said in a low voice that stroked over her skin in a silken caress. Her nipples didn't stand a chance against that voice. And her sex just gave up the fight. "Because I'm weak. I've tried to give you space today, but I wanted to see you. Inhale that scent directly from the source that's embedded in my sheets. Touch this body that I can still feel on my hands. I needed to look in your eyes and see if you regretted taking me inside you."

Taking me inside you.

Oh, how her core clenched around those words as if they were his cock. Regrets? Not that. Not when he'd filled her so completely that even now, she felt him. Even now, she wanted more.

"Talk to me." He flipped over her hand, grazed those wicked lips over her palm and, damn, who knew that nerve in the center had a direct line to her sex? "What are you thinking, Eve?"

"No." She cleared her throat. "I don't regret last night. But I would be lying if I didn't say I was worried."

He lifted his head, and his gaze grew hooded, shuttered. She'd known him long enough to recognize when Kenan was hiding something. Disquiet bloomed in her belly.

"Worried? About what?"

"What it means for us." As hard as it was to maintain visual contact with him, she did it. Because she needed to glimpse the truth in his eyes. "Where do we go from here? Are we just fuck buddies? What does this do to our friendship?" She whispered the last question, part of her afraid to hear his answer.

If he said he wanted a "friends with benefits" relationship, that might crush her because she couldn't stand to be treated like one of his other women. They meant more to each other than that—were more to each other than that. But what if they tried for more and it didn't work out? What if they didn't survive adding sex to their relationship? Where would that leave them? Losing Kenan... That would break her.

Her phone vibrated on the coffee table, preventing Kenan from answering and disrupting her spiral of thoughts. Tendrils of relief and frustration whirled within her as she reached for the cell. But one glimpse at the caller ID on the screen and dread replaced it. Her gaze shifted to Kenan, who stared at her with a calm, cool expression. That demeanor didn't fool her, though. He'd seen the name on the phone.

Gavin.

The phone continued to vibrate on her palm as they stared at one another. Kenan obviously expected her to answer it, and it startled her a little that she had no desire to pick it up. As a matter of fact, the only thing she felt was annoyance at the bad timing. Which was even more surprising given Gavin had been her crush since a teenager. But she sent the call to voice mail and set the phone back on the table, never removing her focus from Kenan.

So she didn't miss the flare of astonishment in his eyes.

Followed by heat so bright, so intense, she swore it seared her skin. And she glorified in the burn.

Using the grip he still retained on her hand, he reeled her closer, and she willingly went to him. Perched on her knees, she hovered over him, straddling his thigh. Releasing her hand, he cupped her face, bringing it down to his, allowing her the opportunity to pull away. As if she would deny either of them the pleasure that awaited them.

He took her mouth. Tenderly. Softly.

And it brought tears to her eyes, so she closed them. But she didn't stop him. Didn't demand he take her harder, wilder.

This. After everything they'd both gone through today, they needed this with each other. *From* each other.

Kenan didn't hurry, although under Eve's palm, his heart thundered. He loved her mouth. That was the only description she could apply. He made love to her mouth, sexing it so thoroughly, her hips twisted and bucked in a restless pattern. She ground her sex against his thigh, seeking relief from the lust coursing through her like a swollen spring flood. Her fingers clawed at his shoulders, and she pressed her chest to his, not caring if he felt the diamond stiffness of her nipples. She had zero shame. Want had taken full control, and modesty had left the building.

Covering his hands with hers, she lowered them from her face and, leaning backward, trailed them down to her aching breasts. Their twin moans inundated the room as his palms molded her, shaped her, relearned her. And when his strong fingers plucked at her nipples, she tossed her head back on her shoulders, arching tighter into his caress.

But, God, it wasn't enough. She grabbed the bottom

of her hoodie and whipped it up and over her head. His growl did things to her, nasty things right between her legs. He cupped her braless breasts again and captured a beaded tip between his lips, his tongue circling her, tugging, sucking. And every stroke and pull echoed over the pulsing button of flesh at the top of her sex.

Oh, God, she could come from this. Just explode from his mouth on her nipple and his thick erection on her core.

When Kenan switched to the neglected mound, his fingers teasing the wet peak, she fluttered her fingers over the smattering of freckles decorating the crests of his cheeks. Then lowered her hands to grip his cock through his pants. The almost feral rumble in his chest ratcheted up her hunger to feed on him as he did her.

Urgency rippled through her, and she scrambled off him, ducking his grasping hands. But when she slid to the floor, kneeling between his legs, his complaint snapped off, his thighs going rigid.

"Sweetheart." He thrust his fingers through her hair, dislodging the bun on top of her head. Blunt nails scraped over her scalp, and she shivered, her own nails biting into the dense muscles of his legs. "This what you want?"

She worked the closure open and the zipper down, then dipped her hand into his black boxer briefs, closing her fist around his hard, hot dick. They both shook and moaned. Damn, he filled her palm to overflowing. Thick. Long. Beautiful. And hers.

Only once she'd pulled him free and stroked her hand down to the base of him, then back up, swallowing the plum-shaped tip in her tight fist, did she glance up and meet his glazed, burning stare.

"You have no idea," she whispered, bending her head and swiping her tongue over the head, tasting his salty, delicious flavor. His hips bucked, sliding a bit more of his length into her mouth, and she took him, sucking gently before sliding him free. "I want all of you."

Let him read whatever he wanted into that. Not like she knew for certain, either.

Closing her eyes, she set about driving them both wild.

Over and over, she swallowed him down. Licking, sucking, teasing, she worshipped him, accepting each grunt and groan and hoarse word of praise as her due. And when he grasped her head, holding her still as he drove into her mouth, using her for his pleasure, she exulted in it. Opening herself wide for him, glorying in each thrust, each plunge, each nudge to the back of her throat.

"Fuck," he snarled, his hands gripping her hair as he breached her throat, slipping into the narrow channel. "Not here. But, goddammit, I will."

He curled his fingers under her shoulders and yanked her back onto the couch, slamming his mouth onto hers. With hurried movements, he stripped her lounge pants from her, leaving her naked and shivering. In the next several moments, he had his shirt over his head, his pants and shoes off and a condom rolled down his dick. Sitting back on the sofa, he cradled her hip and guided her over him. As soon as her thighs bracketed his, he gripped his erect flesh and pressed it to her folds.

Their harsh, fast pants punched the air as she slowly sank down on him.

A keening, sharp cry climbed the back of her throat, but she clenched her teeth, trapping it. In this position, he seemed bigger, thicker. And she breathed through her nose, inhaling deeply and pausing to grant her sex time to accommodate him.

She was stretched so far, packed so full, she could feel him everywhere.

Bowing her head, she pressed her mouth to his forehead, her arms encircling his shoulders, and she clung to him.

"You're so tight, sweetheart. So wet, hot and perfect for me." He pressed a kiss to the hollow of her throat, his arms banded around her waist. "Utterly perfect."

A whimper escaped her, and she circled her hips, pulsing them to claim more of him. With each inch she took, a fierce joy pierced her, along with a wild, raw pleasure. Oh, damn, she didn't know if she could survive this. And when the length of him finally, finally filled her, she admitted to herself that while physically she would come out on the other side of this, emotionally…?

No. She was a goner.

"There you go," he soothed, rubbing his big palms up and down her back, praising her, his ragged chuckle another caress on her cheek. "Look at you, sweetheart, taking all of me. So fucking beautiful and sweet."

She was. For him, she was. And as she rose up, up,

up his cock and plunged back down, tearing a gasp out of both of them, she was also fierce and powerful, too.

She rode him hard, giving him no quarter and offering none to herself. In the furious pace, pleasure careened through her, transforming her into a carnal creature that in parts thrilled and terrified her. She could forget that Kenan hadn't answered the question about where they went from here, about what they were to each other.

She could forget everything but the ecstasy threatening to implode and leave her in so many pieces, she might never be the same.

And yet, she didn't care. She fucked him, racing for that ending, dragging him along with her. She didn't wait for him to take them there. Crushing her mouth to his, she plunged her tongue between his lips, claiming his kiss. Then she reached between them and circled the stiff nub of nerve-packed flesh. Once, twice.

That was all it required to soar over the edge, taking him with her.

Her core clamped down on him, milking, rippling. She flung back her head, crying out his name. Dimly, she heard him shout hers, felt the hard, almost brutal strokes inside her before his arms clinched her to him.

Together, they fell.

And whatever else might happen, they'd catch each other.

Eleven

Kenan studied his computer monitor and the email that filled it.

It was Monday afternoon, almost two days since Gavin had called him to that meeting with him and his parents, and Kenan hadn't reached out to them. Even though his talk with Eve had soothed some of the rawer edges, the pain hadn't disappeared.

I'm ashamed of you.

No matter how hard he tried, he couldn't evict those four words from his head. They taunted him, berated him. And call him a coward, but he hadn't contacted his parents because hearing more of their disappointment, or their rejection, would devastate him.

Yet Gavin, ever the peacemaker, had already done what Kenan and his parents couldn't. Because Kenan hadn't answered his brother's texts or calls, Gavin had emailed, apologizing for setting him up and for what their mother had said. There'd been no way Gavin could've known the meeting would go so left, but Kenan would be lying if he didn't admit he felt a little betrayed that Gavin hadn't given him a heads-up about the subject of the conversation. About them wanting him to return to the company. At least Kenan could've been prepared.

No... Closing out the email, Kenan sighed and reclined back in his chair. He wasn't ready to tackle that yet.

And then there existed the lingering remnants of guilt and jealousy toward Gavin over Eve. Guilt because Kenan was sleeping with the woman Gavin was interested in. Hell, Gavin had called Eve just before they'd had sex Saturday night. That had been awkward as fuck.

But not as awkward as Kenan's reaction to her picking up that phone and waiting to see if she would answer it. Or Kenan on the verge of demanding she not answer it. Begging her not to answer it.

Disgusted with himself, he rubbed his eyes hard with his thumb and forefinger.

Since Saturday, he'd been in Eve's bed, or she'd been in his. Regardless, he'd been inside her. But neither of them had broached the conversation she'd attempted about the status of their relationship. Maybe because she didn't want to know. He couldn't speak for her.

But in the last couple of months, he must've developed a latent cowardice gene because he damn sure didn't want to touch the subject.

Shit, who was he kidding? When it came to Eve, he'd always been a coward.

And though she'd let him have her body, entrusted her pleasure into his hands, nothing had changed. He was still too scared to admit his feelings for her. Even though she'd appeared to choose him over Gavin on Saturday, he was still too insecure over whether he was just a stand-in for his brother. He couldn't forget how many years she'd pined for Gavin. Those feelings didn't just evaporate in days. What would happen when she saw Gavin in person again? Would the love, the need, return? Leaving Kenan where?

Broken.

He didn't trust this…whatever he and Eve had. Especially with it being so new. Not even a week old. How the hell could he trust it, believe it would last, when it was up against a love she'd possessed for years. And with his family already slipping away from him, he couldn't lose Eve, too. So, yeah, he'd gladly be that coward and avoid the "what are we?" conversation. If it allowed him more time with her—touching her, kissing her, going to sleep buried inside her—then he'd duck it like a game of dodgeball. Because that was the selfish bastard he was.

Maybe he'd inherited something from Barron Farrell after all, besides his eyes.

A knock on his door interrupted his thoughts, and he glanced up from blindly staring at his computer screen to see Achilles enter his office.

"Hey," Achilles said. "Bad time?"

"No, not at all. Great timing actually. You can save me from myself."

His brother emitted a low grunt in response, stepping inside and closing the door behind him.

"Anything I can help with?"

A smile tugged at Kenan's mouth in spite of the circumstances. Only months ago, his older brother by months would've never issued that offer. A closed-off, broody giant, the man had had one aim—finish his time at Farrell and get the hell out of Boston. But he'd ended up falling in love with Mycah and bonding with Cain and Kenan, and though Achilles would never be warm and cuddly, he'd definitely come a long way. As evidenced by his question of concern.

Damn. This might mean Kenan couldn't tease him anymore about suffering from middle-child syndrome.

Nah. Where would be the fun in that?

"No, I'm good." When Achilles arched an eyebrow, Kenan grinned. "Wow. Has Mycah been taking you to those childbirth classes again? I'm getting daddy vibes right now."

Achilles pinned him with a grim stare that promised all kinds of bodily injury.

"Fine, fine. I take it back. No daddy vibes." Kenan snickered, holding up his hands. "But if you ask me about my feelings or try to pat me on the back, you're getting side-eye."

"And here I am, sorry for even asking the question."

Kenan laughed. "I'm kidding." But he didn't even attempt to tone down his grin. "What's going on?"

Achilles held up a manila folder. "I have some information on your adoption."

That took care of his amusement. His smile ebbed, falling away completely. And though excitement should've surged inside him, instead a dark sense of foreboding eddied in his chest. He couldn't tear his eyes from that folder, even as he rose from his chair and rounded the desk.

"Kenan?"

"Yes, I'm okay," he murmured, then shifted his gaze to his brother. "Tell me."

Achilles nodded. "I tracked down the lawyer that supposedly handled your adoption. I say supposedly because, Kenan…" He paused, an emotion that deepened the fear in his stomach flashing in Achilles's eyes. "Without betraying confidential information, he revealed that he didn't handle the adoption for your parents. The papers they allowed you to see were falsified."

Falsified.

The word boomed in his head over and over, growing louder and louder. What did that mean?

"Kenan, are you with me?" Achilles moved closer, his hand outstretched toward him.

"I'm good." He nodded. "What else?"

Achilles studied him then jerked his chin. "I kept digging, thinking maybe an attorney with a similar first or last name or maybe a different spelling could've handled the adoption. Maybe it was a mistake on the paperwork. But I couldn't find anything. And that's the issue. There was nothing to find. No filings for Nathan and Dana Rhodes adopting a newborn baby boy. And I've spent months on this, Kenan, but nothing."

Kenan shook his head, frowning. Achilles had been his last hope. His brother was a tech genius. If he couldn't unearth any information, then Kenan didn't have any hope left of finding out the identity of his birth mother.

"Don't worry about it, Achilles," Kenan said, fighting past his disappointment. "You did your best, and I appreciate it. I guess I'll need to find a way to let this go now."

There was a twinge of sadness across Achilles's face, and he closed the distance separating them, gripping Kenan's shoulder.

"No, you don't need to let it go." Achilles stared into his eyes, holding his gaze before he handed him the folder. But he didn't drop his hand from his shoulder. "I promised you I would give you answers. And I wasn't stopping until I could."

Don't take it. Walk away and don't take it.

A voice yelled the warning in his head, and his heart hurled itself against his rib cage. The violent beat echoed in his head, deafening him even as it pumped adrenaline through his body. An acrid taste coated his tongue and bile roiled in his gut. Yet, he still reached for the folder, accepted it.

He flipped it open and scanned the lone document within. A birth certificate. *His* birth certificate.

"How did you…?" He glanced up at his brother, confusion swirling in his head. "My parents told me this had been sealed with the adoption."

Achilles shook his head, and Kenan dropped his gaze back to the printout, studying it with eager, greedy eyes.

Child.

Kenan Anthony Rhodes.

He frowned. Rhodes? Why would his adoptive last name be on his birth certificate?

Father.

Blank.

Not a shock there. Barron Farrell wouldn't have agreed to have his name recorded.

Mother.

Dana Rhodes.

"Dana…" He choked. Stumbled backward. Or he would've if Achilles's hold on his shoulder hadn't prevented him from falling. All the while, his grip on the folder and the printout didn't ease up. "Dana," he rasped again. "What…?"

It couldn't be. This had to be a lie.

Pain blasted him, stealing his air, his strength, his ability to think.

"I'm sorry, Kenan," Achilles whispered.

The pain in his brother's voice, the grief in his eyes. They confirmed what his numb mind couldn't grasp.

His adopted mother was his birth mother.

Twelve

Eve stood outside the break room at Rhodes Realty, twisting her fingers in front of her.

"Really?" she muttered, forcing her hands to her sides.

This was her mother. She'd never been scared to talk to her mother before. Nervous maybe, but not scared.

But you've never insulted and hurt her so deeply before, either.

Dammit. She really had to find a muzzle for her subconscious.

Yolanda had asked for time, and since Eve had been the one to inflict the harm, she should really allow her mother to determine the length of that time and space. But it was late Monday afternoon, and Yolanda had yet to reach out to her. Eve couldn't allow this wound to fester; she needed to try to heal this rift.

And approaching her mother at her job lessened the chances of her mother going off on her.

Inhaling a deep breath, Eve pushed open the glass door, silently thanking God for her mother's predictability with her late-afternoon cup of coffee.

"Hey, Mom."

Yolanda glanced up from the coffee maker, and though Eve expected to see surprise in her expression, it didn't appear. A faint, wry smile twisted her mouth.

"You don't seem shocked to see me here," Eve said.

Her mother arched an eyebrow, hitting a button and filling the room with the scent of fresh, brewing coffee.

"You're my daughter. I wouldn't have given you more than a few days before I sought you out, either, if there was discord between us. And—" she shrugged a shoulder "—Mr. Leonard called and let me know you were on your way up."

Eve smothered a snort. Right.

A tense silence fell that carried a hint of awkwardness.

God, she detested it. This wasn't them. They'd never been uneasy with each other. Since this was her fuckup, it fell on her to fix it. In any way she could.

It helped that her mother didn't seem as angry as she'd been Saturday. But that hurt… The hurt still lingered in her eyes, and Eve would do anything to erase it.

"Mom, I'm sorry I lied to you. Because I can call it keeping a secret or just not telling you, but it comes down to that one thing—I lied to you. For four years. And I'm so sorry."

"*Why*, Eve?" Yolanda leaned a hip against the counter, rubbing her hands together then crossing her arms. For a woman who was the epitome of composure, the fidgety movements screamed volumes. Guilt swam in Eve's chest. "I've gone over and over the other night. And all I can come up with is, for some reason, you were afraid to tell me. And if that's true, then I'm to blame. I've done something that prohibited you—"

"No, Mom." Eve rushed forward, cupping her mother's upper arms. "No. This is on me. All on me." Releasing her mother, she pressed her fingertips to her mouth, searching for the words to explain a mindset that she'd battled with her entire life. "All my life I've watched you work hard, often struggle, to provide for us. For me. And I never wanted to do anything to render that struggle a wasted effort. So I put my everything into school, into a career that would make you proud. My one fear in this world is disappointing you… or shaming you. Teaching was something you could tell your friends, coworkers and pastor about. Your daughter designing underwear and selling it? That's not something you could proudly share."

"And why not?" her mother scoffed, slicing a hand through the air. "What? I don't wear underwear?"

"Mom. You've never approved of me taking art. Then there's the instability of it as a job. And your being an elder in the church. What would your members say if they knew your daughter sold lingerie?"

"Oh, I suppose because we worship Jesus, we don't like sexy panties?"

"Mom, I'm being serious!"

"So am I." Yolanda threw up her hands, heaving a loud sigh that reeked of her exasperation. And possibly love. "Baby, let me explain why I was so angry. I'm your mother first before anything else. And as your mother, you didn't allow me the opportunity to brag about you, to celebrate milestones with you. To comfort and be there for you during setbacks. That's my job as a mom. I felt like I failed you in some way, when all I've ever wanted to be is your cheerleader and your safe place."

"You have been," Eve whispered.

"No, I haven't been," she disagreed just as softly. "And regardless of what you're saying, that's on me. Somewhere, somehow, I gave you the impression that you had to prove yourself to me. That my love was based on works instead of you being you. And that's just not true. I love you. I'm proud of you. Did I worry that if you chose a difficult career that you'd struggle? Yes. I didn't want that for you. I wanted more. But, baby, that's what parents do. We want better for our children than we had. But even worrying, I would've supported you with your lingerie company. Shoot, I would've given you money, been support staff, anything you needed, because I want you to succeed in all you do. You, Eve, are my greatest joy and accomplishment. And if you're happy—whether that's teaching, operating a lingerie company or picking up garbage off the side of the highway—then that's all that matters. I'm going to be there for you, in your corner. Although, we're going to have a long conversation about the garbage picking and the career trajectory in that."

Laughter burst from Eve, along with tears. Unable to hold back any longer, she threw her arms around her mother. Yolanda's arms closed around her, and they held one another tight. Saturday night, that weight hadn't disappeared from her chest. But today, it did. She could breathe. Her heart was lighter.

She was...free.

Laughing again, she squeezed her mother, then leaned back. Tears glistened in Yolanda's eyes, too, as she smiled at Eve.

"So-o-o... Does this mean you want free samples?"

Yolanda arched an eyebrow. "Of course. What's the point of having a daughter who's a businesswoman if I don't get free stuff?"

Their snickers filled the breakroom.

Twenty minutes later, Eve pushed out of the office building onto the sidewalk. Smiling, she turned her face up into the late-afternoon sun, embracing the last of its rays.

"Oof."

She jerked up her hands, bracing herself as she slammed into a hard surface. Or a hard chest, she realized, when strong hands clasped her arms, steadying her.

"Hey, stranger."

Glancing up, she met Gavin's dark brown gaze and beautiful smile. She stilled, waiting for that familiar warm, melting desire that the sight of him brought.

For years, it'd encompassed her, but now, standing in his embrace…

Nothing.

Nothing except for a twinge of guilt for leading him on and perhaps a little sadness because Gavin was such a good man. And, dammit, it would've been less complicated for her to love him instead of her best friend.

"Hi, Gavin." She smiled, stepping back out of his hold. "It's good to see you."

"You, too."

His gaze dropped down over her, and in spite of her newfound revelation regarding her lack of feelings toward him, she still blushed. Because, well, a handsome man had just checked her out. She was in love with another man, not dead—

Holy shit. She was in love with Kenan.

She'd loved him for years. But *in* love with him?

Terror streaked through her, screaming like a freight train on greased wheels and no breaks.

This wasn't good. Oh, God, this *so* wasn't good.

For her, the transition wasn't shocking. She'd meant it when she'd told him he was the best man she knew. No man had ever understood her, supported her, believed in her…loved her like him. And since she'd never been one to indulge in casual sex, she couldn't have separated her feelings when they became lovers. That couldn't be said of Kenan, though. Yes, they were intimately involved, but he'd never expressed wanting anything more than friendship. Unlike her, he was the king of casual sex, and just because he'd been inside her—repeatedly—didn't mean he'd suddenly developed deeper feelings for her.

Her stomach bottomed out, her heart thudding.

What did this mean for them? Because if he rejected her... Would she survive that? Would their friendship survive that? She didn't know if she could be around him, loving him, when he didn't feel the same way. It would hurt too much.

"Eve?" Gavin cupped her elbow, and she jerked her gaze back to him from over his shoulder, where it'd wandered. "Are you okay?"

"Yes." She exhaled a trembling breath, shaken by her self-revelation. "I'm fine. I'm sorry, what were you saying?"

He cocked his head, studying her. "I was saying, I called the other night to see if you were free this weekend. I'd love to take you out on another date."

Regret tightened her stomach. Considering what she'd just admitted to herself, she hated having to reject someone.

"Gavin, you're incredibly kind and sweet, and I really enjoyed our date, but I'm sorry. I have to say no. I can't this weekend. Or any other weekend. I—"

He squeezed her elbow, cutting off her explanation. "Let me guess," he said, a wry smile curving his mouth. "Kenan."

Her lips parted on a soft gasp. Was she so transparent? Damn, how pathetic.

"How did you...?"

"How did I know? I might be a little slow on the

uptake but looking back on it, you two have always been very close."

"We've been friends for a long time."

"Okay, but the way my brother has looked at you is not very...friendly." He shook his head. "And neither was that kiss at the club, regardless of the story he spun for me. If I hadn't wanted to get to know you so badly, I would've dug deeper into that explanation instead of just accepting it on its face, but..." He shrugged. "The signs have been there. Kenan's been in love with you for a very long time. So while I'm disappointed, I'm not shocked."

"You're wrong about that." Oh, how she wished he wasn't, but he couldn't be more wrong. "That really was an act that night just to get your attention." She winced. "This *thing* between your brother and me— it's new."

His mouth tightened, and she had the impression he was fighting back a smile.

"Okay."

She narrowed her eyes on him, but after a moment, huffed out a chuckle. Then, sobering, she said, "Gavin, I'm sorry. I didn't mean to—"

"No apologies necessary, Eve." He pulled her into his arms, hugging her. "If anyone deserves happiness, it's my brother. And he deserves you." He brushed a kissed over her cheek.

"Well, this is sweet."

Eve jerked out of Gavin's arms, whirling around to face Kenan. His beautiful, frigid gaze roamed over her before shifting over her shoulder to Gavin. The stern, forbidding lines of his face didn't soften as he smiled. If anything, his expression hardened.

"Please, don't let me interrupt," he said in that same, pleasant voice that carried a bitter undertone.

"Kenan, this isn't..." She trailed off. Jesus, she couldn't utter that cliché.

But he didn't have a problem finishing it.

Arching an eyebrow, he drawled, "It isn't what it looks like? Really? C'mon, Eve, you can do better than that."

"Kenan," Gavin murmured. "Take advice from your brother. The brother you've been avoiding. Don't fuck this up." Squeezing her shoulder, he said, "Goodbye, Eve."

Gavin walked off, entering the office building and leaving her and Kenan alone. Well, as alone as they could be on a busy sidewalk.

"Kenan," she began, "I know how that looked, but honestly, there's nothing going on between me and Gavin. Actually, we were talking about—"

"Let me guess. This is a case of believing you or my lying eyes, right?" He let loose a harsh chuckle that abraded her skin. "Sorry, sweetheart. I'm not that gullible. Or rather, I'm through being that naive."

Confused, she frowned. What did that even mean? Taking a step toward him, she ignored the people teeming around them, focusing only on the man—her best friend, the man she loved with her whole heart— before her. The man who currently looked at her as if he didn't know her...and didn't care to.

"Kenan, if you'd only listen to me. I just happened

to bump into Gavin. I was here to see my mom, and I ended up talking to him. Nothing other than that happened between us."

"Other than a kiss, Eve."

He glanced away from her, but not before she glimpsed the slip of his hard mask and the tortured expression that replaced it. Her hands jerked to her chest, pressed there over her aching heart. What the hell was going on? There was more here than him being angry about what he *thought* he'd witnessed.

"Kenan—" she whispered.

"No," he interrupted, voice as cold as a winter wind sweeping over Boston Harbor. "I'm through blindly accepting lies. I'm done being someone's secret and their Plan B. Never again."

"I don't know what the hell that's supposed to mean," she said, her hands fisting over her chest, desperation and anger curdling inside her. Deliberately, she stretched out her fingers and stared down at them, as if she could literally see her future with this man slipping through them. Yet, she tried. She *fought*. For him. For them. "I've never lied to you, and you've never been a secret for me. I've never been ashamed of you, never hid you. And I don't even understand what a Plan B means. Kenan, you've been my best friend and— and…" She swallowed, shifted closer to him, slid her hands up his abdomen to his chest until her palms covered his heart. Hope crashed inside her at the heavy, wild beat under her hand. "And I love you, Kenan. Yes, as my friend, but also as more. As the man who makes me whole, gives me joy, is the other half of my heart. I love you."

The air stalled in her lungs, and her pulse echoed in her ears, that hope, so fragile yet strong in its will to grow, beating, waiting. But as she stared at his shuttered, aloof face, it died a slow, excruciating death.

The pain in her chest expanded, though, threatening to explode until she sucked in a breath. She stumbled backward, and Kenan reached for her, but she batted away his hands, not able to bear his touch. His rejection.

"You don't believe me," she rasped.

"Maybe the kiss was platonic." His eyes dipped to her mouth, and for a moment, she caught a flicker of heat in the bright depths, igniting that traitorous hope again. But when he returned his gaze to hers, the emptiness there gutted her. "But in love with me? No. How could you be when not just weeks ago, I was helping you try to win my brother because you were in love with him? He's had your heart for years, Eve. Years. Now suddenly I'm supposed to believe it's mine?" His mouth twisted into a hard—cruel—caricature of a smile. "No, I'm not that lucky. Not that willing to believe in fairy tales anymore."

She shouldn't be able to still stand on her feet. Still breathe. Shouldn't be able to exist under so much pain. Part of her needed to pound on his chest, demand he fight along with her for not just who they were but who they could be. But the other half? That half had perhaps seen this coming, and she protected herself.

Wrapped herself in the remnants of pride she had left that she refused to sacrifice at his feet.

Yes, she loved him, but she also loved herself.

More importantly, she *valued* herself.

"I can't make you believe me, and I can't force you to accept a love I'd freely give you without any strings attached. But if there's one thing that you, yourself, taught me, it's that love is a gift. Loyalty is earned. My love for you is yours because it's mine to give, not for you to determine who it belongs to. And despite what you think, you've more than earned my loyalty, which means I'd never lie to you, never betray you. So for you to believe differently is on you, not me."

She inhaled a shuddering breath, unable to believe after all these years, this was how their friendship would end. On a busy street. Because he couldn't get past his own issues to see her. To love her.

"In spite of us introducing sex into our relationship, I thought we were close enough that you could come to me with whatever is going on with you. Maybe we were wrong to go there with each other because I've lost you to whatever demons have always chased you."

"I don't know what you're talking about."

She shook her head, smiling, having no doubt it reflected the soul-deep sadness that hollowed her out. Because try as she might, she couldn't conjure up anger toward him. Not when she understood him more than he understood himself. Not when she loved him so much.

"It all comes down to fear, Kenan. You're afraid to trust that I could possibly love you. That I could prefer you over Gavin. How could I when you've always believed your parents never have? You can't accept that you're so special, so beautiful, that loving you is as easy as breathing. So you're pushing me away out of fear." She spread her hands wide, palms up. "I can't make you believe that I love you, that I want only you, because that would require you believing in yourself. That would mean you'd have to extend a trust to me that's beyond you. As a friend? Yes. But with your heart? With the possibility of perhaps hurting you? No. And that saddens me, Kenan. Because you deserve more than that. But when it comes down to it, your fear and your insecurities broke us. And that's something you'll have to live with."

Not giving him a chance to reply—a chance to utter one more word that might score another hit that could devastate her further—she turned and walked away.

Walked away from him, but toward herself.

Thirteen

Kenan stared out the window of his home study, not really seeing the private, walled-in garden in the back of his home. He fisted his fingers inside his pants pockets, his hands feeling a little empty without the ever-present glass tumblers that had been in them since Achilles's bomb and the later sidewalk confrontation with Eve. He'd spent all that Monday evening and Tuesday drunk. Wednesday, he'd crawled out of the bottle, but he hadn't returned to the office, calling in ill. Not that it was a lie. He was sick.

Heartsick.

Soul sick.

If that wasn't a thing, it should be.

Sighing, he rubbed a hand over his head, dragging it down his face and chin. Scruff from the last couple of days scraped his palm, and it reminded him that he needed to shave before he returned to the office tomorrow. Because he had to return. He couldn't hide out in his home nursing his open wounds forever. No matter how much he longed to. The thought of facing anyone right now had him longing to open another bottle of Scotch.

Facing anyone?

More specifically, Eve. Every time he closed his eyes, an image of her on that sidewalk saying she loved him wavered on his eyelids. Her voice rang in his head, and he couldn't escape himself. Couldn't escape her.

I love you, Kenan. Yes, as my friend, but also as more. As the man who makes me whole, gives me joy, is the other half of my heart.

When it comes down to it, your fear and your insecurities broke us. And that's something you'll have to live with.

No amount of alcohol could shut out those words. Words that followed him into sleep, so he didn't. They tortured him, condemned him. Because she'd spoken truth. He couldn't believe she loved him, chose him over Gavin. And, yes, it did come down to his own fears and insecurities. Yet, he couldn't shake them. But, God, he wanted to. Didn't she know he yearned to believe her? To be able to claim her as his, and to be claimed by her in return?

But like he'd told her, he'd ceased to be a dreamer, a believer in fairy tales, in happily-ever-afters. As soon as he'd read the birth certificate in that folder, it'd been drilled home for him that this world was hard, cold and a place of lies.

So he'd rather let her go than risk her brutalizing his heart when she walked away later.

If that made him a coward, then so be it.

His doorbell echoed through his house, and he closed his eyes. He could ignore it and maybe whoever it was, who'd shown up uninvited, would go away. Several seconds passed, and the tension eased from his body.

The doorbell rang again. And again.

"Shit."

Sighing, he exited the study. Only three people would be so bold to lean on his doorbell and refuse to leave. One of them had walked away from him a few days ago, cutting him out of her life. The other two were bound to show up at some point. He was actually surprised it'd taken either of them this long.

Opening the front door, he met Achilles's familiar, patient gaze.

Without a word, Kenan shifted backward, allowing his brother to enter.

"Beer? Water? Whiskey?" Kenan offered, walking into the kitchen.

"Beer's good." Achilles leaned back against the counter, crossing his arms as if there for a casual visit instead of an intervention.

After pulling open the refrigerator door and removing one for himself, as well, Kenan passed his brother a brown bottle. They twisted off the caps and drank in silence, facing each other across the kitchen.

Lowering the beer after a long pull, Kenan cocked his head, peering at his brother.

"Go on and say it. Get it over with."

Achilles nodded but didn't immediately reply. He tilted the bottle, downed another gulp. "Have you talked to your mother yet?"

Kenan barked out a sharp laugh. "Jumping right into it, are we?" He shook his head, setting the bottle behind him on the counter. "No, I haven't talked to her yet."

"Why not?"

"Because I don't trust myself. I'm too fucking angry. And she's still my mother, and I won't disrespect her."

Achilles nodded again. "I understand that. When I first went to jail, I was so angry with my mother. Because it'd been her boyfriend. Because she'd brought him home. Because it hadn't been the first shithead she'd dated. And then I felt so much guilt because I was blaming the victim. And she was my mother. I loved her. The only person I had. But I realized I could be both. Mad and still adore her. The important thing is love always wins out."

A ball of emotions—the very emotions Achilles spoke of—lodged in Kenan's throat, rendering it impossible for him to speak. He picked up his bottle again and tried to drink the blockage down.

"But there's something else, isn't there?" Achilles asked quietly. "Something else that has you upset. And—" he arched an eyebrow "—rough?"

Kenan snorted. "If by 'rough' you mean 'look like shit,' then thank you for being diplomatic."

He stared down at the floor. Did he really want

to go into it? Not really. But then Achilles had gone through hell with Mycah. If anyone would understand, he would. And, well… Achilles was his brother. Not long ago, Kenan had willingly been there for Achilles. Obviously, Achilles wanted to do the same for him. So Kenan would let him.

"Yeah. Yeah, there is something else," Kenan admitted.

Then he spilled everything.

About approaching Eve about the Bromberg's proposal.

Their deal regarding Gavin.

The turn in their relationship.

Finding her and Gavin together, and her declaration of love.

His rejection.

He even confessed about how this proposal was his way of proving himself at Farrell. Proving himself worthy to be there.

Achilles shoved off the counter, slowly straightening to his full height, which topped Kenan by a couple of inches. "We'll get to Eve in a minute, but let's tackle the Farrell thing first. Are you fucking with me?" he demanded. "That was my hang-up, not yours. If anyone belongs there, besides Cain, it's you. And you are more than worthy to be there, just like Cain, just like me. This proposal doesn't determine that. These next few months don't. You are enough. And fuck those who don't know it."

Kenan blinked. Cleared his throat.

"You must be taking pep-talk lessons from Cain," he rasped.

"I took notes." Achilles's grin flashed in his thick beard before he dipped his chin, studying him. "You know what I went through with Mycah. How I almost allowed my past to dictate my future with her. I let it color how I saw myself and my own worth. And I nearly lost Mycah. I nearly lost you and Cain."

Achilles cupped Kenan's shoulder, squeezing it.

"If you don't talk with your parents and deal with this fear that's eating away at you, you'll lose Eve. I grew up in a house that didn't have much, but I never doubted how much I was loved. I don't have that burden, Kenan. And I'm so sorry you do. No child should ever feel second in their parents' love. But one thing I can guarantee you, because I've been around you and Eve, you have never been second with her. Your welfare, your happiness. *You*. Accept that, Kenan. Because she's right. You need to be brave enough to risk your heart. And there's no safer bet than her."

The cold of the beer bottle numbed Kenan's palms and fingers.

They were the only things numb on him. Everything else—his chest, his stomach, his head, hell, even his legs—hurt, throbbed. Almost as if all his limbs had been deadened, and all of him had come back online at once. He tingled, his skin prickled.

Because he was alive.

All his life, he hadn't felt like he'd belonged in his family. He had the last name, but not the acceptance.

Now he understood why. And that wasn't on him. It'd never been on him. And yet, it'd ruled him.

It'd even prevented him from telling Eve he loved her all these years. Because he feared her rejection. Feared she couldn't possibly see him as more than a friend, see more in him to love because his mother and father didn't.

Because he didn't.

Yet, Eve had been the one person in his life who'd unconditionally offered him acceptance, affirmation, forgiveness…love. She'd always given him love.

I love you, Kenan. Yes, as my friend, but also as more. As the man who makes me whole, gives me joy, is the other half of my heart.

When he'd replayed that in his head earlier, it'd brought him pain.

Now it brought him a cautious joy.

It brought him hope.

Could he reach for that future with her? Grab hold of the happiness that could be theirs?

He wanted to be brave enough to. He wanted to be the man she needed. Whom she deserved. Was that man him? He didn't know. But she'd chosen him, and he damn sure would never make her regret it.

That is if he could convince her to forgive him for hurting her and give him another chance.

Damn.

He was going to need a miracle.

Or maybe… He lifted his head and met Achilles's steady gaze.

Just maybe a little help from family.

Fourteen

The early afternoon sun beamed down on Kenan's head and shoulders, and he basked in it as he stared out over the pond in Boston Public Garden. With the warmer weather, the ducks and a couple of swans had returned. Tourists, as well as some locals, pedaled swan boats around the water, while a guide regaled them with facts about the city and the park that sat right in the middle of it. This had been one of his favorite places when he'd been a kid. His mother had brought him here often, and they'd feed the ducks, he'd hang off the statues and they'd just spend time together. Those were some of his happiest memories.

It's why he'd asked her to meet him here.

Nerves played a brutal game of kickball with his stomach. Since calling his mother the evening before, after his talk with Achilles, he'd been going over and over in his head what he intended to say to her. How to broach the subject of being lied to about his very identity for his entire life. How to ask why his own mother didn't want to claim him as her own…

He still didn't know.

Part of him would have preferred to avoid this and her. But he couldn't go to Eve, have a healthy future with her, if he didn't confront his past.

For her, he'd do anything.

"Kenan."

He turned to face his mother, his hands sliding into his pants pockets. An ache caused twinges and spasms in his chest. She looked the same—beautifully dressed, carefully composed, a professional, older, wealthy woman. But he looked at her with new eyes. He saw the shape of her mouth and cheekbones, which they shared. He might have Barron's eye color, but the shape of those eyes belonged to her. Why hadn't he noticed all of this before?

Because he hadn't been looking. He hadn't been seeking himself in the face of his adoptive mother. But now, with newfound knowledge, he spied himself in his birth mother.

"Mom."

She didn't come closer to kiss him on his cheek, and he didn't move near to offer. Instead, they stood, facing each other like long-ago gunslingers. Instead of guns, though, they wielded lies and truth.

"We haven't been here together in a long time," she murmured. "I see Romeo and Juliet have returned."

She hiked her chin toward the two swans in the pond named after the Shakespearean couple. "Somehow, though, I don't think you asked me here to visit Boston's favorite couple and a trip down memory lane."

"No, I didn't." A jumble of frustration, anger, love and pain rolled inside of him. He couldn't begin to untangle them, so he embraced them, as Achilles had suggested. Trusting that love would win out. "I needed to talk to you, and this place that holds good memories for both of us seemed like a safe place."

"We need a safe place?" She laughed, and he caught the jangle of nerves underneath. "That certainly sounds ominous."

"Mom, you and Dad didn't want me to dig into my adoption, but I did." He didn't reveal Achilles's involvement since she already resented his brother because of his relation to Barron. "I found my birth certificate."

He didn't elaborate—didn't need to. Her face blanked in shock before it crumpled, and tears glistened in her eyes. Her fingers fluttered to the base of her throat, and though her lips moved, no words emerged.

"You're my birth mother," he stated, and she didn't deny it. Amazed that his voice remained calm and steady, when inside he yelled until his throat was raw, he continued, "Let me tell you how it was, growing up in our house believing I was adopted and abandoned by a biological mother who didn't want me. I should've felt blessed because I was chosen by our family. Instead, I was an outsider, an interloper. Raised by a father who never could quite successfully pretend to want me as his son. I grew up needing to prove myself worthy of the Rhodes last name, of earning my place in my home because I should be grateful to you and Dad for giving it to me. But no matter what I did, I never could achieve that gold standard. I was never enough simply because of my birth. And all that time—*all that time*—you knew I was yours. And you let me believe otherwise. You refused to claim me. I need to know why."

The tears that had glinted in her eyes streamed down her face. Trembling, she reached into her purse and removed a handkerchief, then blotted at her tears and pressed the cloth to her face, hiding behind it. Kenan didn't rush her, but gave her time to gather herself.

Finally, his mother lifted her head, her mouth trembling.

"I'm sorry, Kenan. I'm so sorry. I didn't mean—" She shuddered out a breath, her shoulders drooping. "No, I won't make excuses. You deserve more than that from me. I owe you the truth." She paused and her gaze shifted to the pond. "Years ago, your father and I… Our marriage was in a bad place. All we did was argue. I felt unloved, he felt unappreciated. It was… rough. During that time, I met Barron Farrell at a dinner party. We were seated next to one another, and he could be very charming. That would've ended there, but a couple of weeks later, we bumped into one another again at a gala. I'm not proud to admit it, but we started a brief affair."

The honking of ducks pockmarked the silence between them as she fell quiet and Kenan studied her stoic expression. Stoic except for the sadness in her gaze. And the shame. His fingers curled into his palms to prevent him from wrapping his arms around her. But he couldn't give that to her right now. Not when a chaotic storm raged inside him.

"I became pregnant, and I swear to you, Kenan—" she jerked her head to him, and her voice lowered, harshened "—I never once considered not having you, regardless of the circumstances of your conception."

"I was a mistake," he said, the words barreling out of him on a bitter wave.

"No." She grabbed his arm, shook it. "No. My affair was a mistake, a betrayal of my vows. But you were not a mistake. You were *mine*. Are mine. You always have been."

You just didn't claim me.

The accusation burned on his tongue, but he doused it, the ashes acrid in his mouth. With a heavy sigh, she dropped her grip on him and wrapped her arms around herself.

"I know my actions contradicted—contradict—my words. I'm not making excuses for myself, but back then, I was so scared. Scared of having another baby by a man who wasn't my husband. Scared to lose my husband and marriage, my family. Barron didn't want anything to do with you. We all know he's good for walking away from his responsibilities with no consequences," she said, anger flickering in her tone. "I had to tell your father the truth, and he was furious, of course. Not only had I cheated on him, but I was pregnant. Still… He wanted to save our marriage. To protect my reputation, he insisted we pretend that we adopted you. That way, I could keep you, raise you and everyone could avoid the pain and damage of a scandal."

"You sacrificed me on the altar of your marriage."

She sucked in a sharp breath, pressing her hands to her chest, but again she didn't deny his statement.

"You sacrificed my identity, my sense of security, my authentic, honest relationships so you and Dad could keep your ideal of a marriage and family. And the sad part? We were never perfect. I grew up with an emotionally distant father, who even as a child I sensed resented me, but I could never pinpoint why. Now I know. Because I was a constant reminder of his wife's affair. He would never appoint me to replace him when he retired because I'm not his son. And he made that abundantly clear without saying the words. And all along you knew why, but let me believe it was in my head. I needed you," he whispered.

"I'm so sorry, Kenan." She lifted her hand and it hovered above his face. When he didn't dodge it, she cradled his cheek. Love and so much pain shone in her eyes that it almost hurt him to meet her damp gaze. "God, you have no idea how many regrets I have. Thirty years' worth. Every day I've woken up deciding to lie to you, to not tell you who I am, has been hell. You're my son, not just by love and choice but by birth and I'm so damn proud of you. I love you." She cupped his other cheek. "Tell me what to do. What you need from me. Admit the truth to everyone? I will. Whatever you need because for the first time this is about you."

He covered her hands with his, bowing his head, tears stinging his eyes. Jesus. The anger flickering inside him demanded she submit a press release in every news-media outlet and expose the truth. But the sadness, the love, the…acceptance and need to just move on didn't require the penance of her blowing up her life, reputation and marriage just to appease his hurt heart.

Where did they go from here? He didn't know. They—him, her, his father—had a lot of healing to do individually and, one day, as a family. And maybe he and Nathan would never be close, but for the first time, the weight of that didn't constrict his chest. Because finally, Kenan understood, it wasn't his burden to bear.

He inhaled a deep, cleansing breath. A lighter breath. They had time to figure it out. And while he couldn't do anything about the pain, disillusionment and anger that still swam inside him, he could offer the one thing he needed in his life—forgiveness.

Drawing her into his arms, he held her. And she clung to him, her sob vibrating through him.

"I forgive you, Mom. I love you."

Fifteen

"This way, Ms. Burke." The older woman who'd introduced herself as Charlene led Eve through the executive offices of Farrell International.

Eve recognized her as Cain Farrell's assistant, although they'd never been formally introduced. Which only deepened Eve's curiosity about why the company CEO's personal assistant was leading her to a mysterious room for a mysterious meeting after an equally mysterious summons downtown.

She'd almost told Cain to forget it. Who cared if he helmed one of the wealthiest, most powerful conglomerates in the world? Her heart littered her chest in itty-bitty pieces. Besides, she'd overnighted the final designs and samples for the proposal to Kenan days ago. She had no more business with him or Farrell. But that rebellion had lasted about ten seconds before she'd conceded and agreed to show up.

As long as she didn't have to meet with Kenan. Cain wouldn't be that cruel...would he? No, she refused to believe that. It'd been a little over a week since she'd last seen Kenan on that sidewalk, and she wasn't ready to change that. Not yet. Eventually, she'd have to face him, but...

She gave her head a small shake, focusing on the arrow-straight spine of the woman in front of her. Curiosity drove her here, but already she itched to leave for her heart and sanity's sake.

"Right in here." She paused before a glass door where closed blinds prevented her from glimpsing inside. "Go on in. They're expecting you." Charlene smiled and cracked open the door.

They? Who in the world was *they*?

Stomach dipping in trepidation, she gave the assistant a tremulous smile in return and slid through the opening. She entered a packed conference room, and a sweep revealed an empty black, leather chair at the very end of the long wood table. She quickly sank into it, her gaze centered on the man standing next to a screen at the front of the room.

Kenan.

Their gazes locked, and a current of electricity pulsed through her, sizzling in her veins. Lust and need had no care for a broken heart and injured pride. All her body and sex knew was that the man who delivered orgasms like he'd invented them stood mere feet from her.

Traitors.

But… Oh, God, she'd missed him.

Everything about him. It was a physical ache, and not all of it sexual. That part of who they were was so new, it didn't encompass even half of what she longed for. She hungered to hear his deep, whiskey smooth voice, breathe in his comforting, earthy scent and feel the security of his tall, powerful body. The security of his arms.

And, yes, she yearned for the devastating pleasure only he could bring her.

Thank God a room full of people separated them. Or else she might do something she'd promised herself she wouldn't—throw herself at him.

Averting her gaze, she scanned the room again, noting Cain, Achilles and his wife toward the head of the table. The other men and women she didn't recognize, but Eve could guess the purpose of this meeting. Kenan's proposal.

Anxiety pooled in her belly again, but this time for him.

Please, God, let him nail it. He deserves this.

"A major component of the rebranding of the Bromberg's chain is modernizing its stores and businesses while still maintaining the class, fashion and lavishness that the department stores are nationally recognized for. We're seeking a fusion of classic and contemporary, while retaining our established customer base and inviting a younger clientele. And, of course, a wider profit margin. Here is just one example of how we plan to accomplish it."

He shifted to the side, and the slide on the screen displayed her pink-and-black logo. Her heart pounded, pride straightening her shoulders even as tension and tendrils of nervousness curled inside her.

"Intimate Curves is an online lingerie boutique that caters exclusively to plus-size women. It also sells lotions, jewelry and other merchandise from local artisans and entrepreneurs. The business has been in operation for four years and has been hugely successful. I've included numbers for the last two years in your file so you can see for yourself. Intimate Curves has not only enjoyed a very healthy profit, but its reputation is also exemplary both regionally and nationally. As a matter of fact, the company was recently the recipient of this year's Small Business Award from the National Association of Women Entrepreneurs."

Warmth flooded her, and under the table she tightly clasped her hands together. She didn't know if anyone else in the conference room could detect the pride in his voice, but she did. God, she did.

"If we go forward with this rebranding, the very talented and gifted owner and designer agreed to provide us with six exclusive designs that won't be for sale anywhere except for the Intimate Curves flagship store. Imagine that. Bromberg's having the only brick-and-mortar boutique with designs that aren't even available online. That kind of exclusivity is guaranteed sales."

"And the owner is fully on board with this?" an older man in a suit that probably cost more than her condo asked, his eyebrow arched.

Kenan's gaze briefly rested on her but shifted away. "Yes, she is."

"Is she going to be the face of the boutique?" the man pressed.

Kenan hesitated. "That hasn't been deter—"

"I will be."

The words escaped Eve before she acknowledged her intention to speak. Or her full decision to reveal her identity. Since the inception of Intimate Curves, she'd hidden behind a logo and a brand out of concern for backlash from her mother, her job. The truth was, she'd used that as an excuse to not fully step out on faith and claim her dream of being a full-time businesswoman.

Staring into Kenan's gleaming eyes, she wasn't afraid anymore.

"I'm sorry to interrupt," she said, glancing around the table before meeting the curious scrutiny of the gentleman who'd first spoken. "My name is Eve Burke, owner and head designer of Intimate Curves. If the re-branding goes through, I will be fully involved with the flagship store, and will continue to provide exclusive designs for the boutique as well as operate my online company."

"Thank you, Eve," Kenan murmured. "As you can see, Intimate Curves is just one example of how we will cultivate new business partnerships while still maintaining established relationships. The plan isn't to alienate our current client base, but to retain them and attract more. And with this marketing plan in place, I believe the chain will be more successful and profitable than ever before."

Kenan continued with his presentation for another fifteen minutes, and when he finished, she barely managed not to break out in spontaneous applause. Barely. Regardless of how things had ended between them romantically, he was first and foremost her best friend, and she, more than anyone, understood what this proposal meant to him.

As the vote on it went forward, she held her breath.

And when the majority of people voted for the rebranding, approving the proposal, the air released from her lungs on a delighted sigh.

Her heart pressed against her sternum, seeming to expand until her chest couldn't contain it. She glanced at Kenan, and as if he'd been waiting on her, his bright gaze captured hers. A slow smile curved his sensual mouth, and she returned it.

Shortly after, the meeting adjourned, and she waited at the back of the room. Congratulate him and leave—that was the plan.

"I believe congratulations are in order to you, too, Ms. Burke," a tall, olive-skinned man said, stopping in front of Eve. Thick, dark hair tumbled over his forehead and framed an indecently lush mouth and solid jaw. Glittering black eyes stared down at her with an intensity that verged on unnerving. "The product, artistry and numbers from your company are impressive."

"Thank you, Mr.…"

He extended a hand toward her, dipping his chin. "Nico Morgan. Minor shareholder in Farrell and future investor in the Bromberg's project." A faint smile flirted with his mouth, but it didn't reach those onyx eyes. And as she shook his hand, a shiver tripped down her spine. "I look forward to a great partnership, Ms. Burke."

Nodding again, he released her and exited the office. She stared after him for a moment, then shook her head. He was *intense*.

"Eve? Can we talk for a minute?" A warm, big hand wrapped around hers, and the crackle that rippled up her arm and sizzled across her breasts telegraphed who touched her before she turned around.

Briefly closing her eyes, she pivoted and offered Kenan a polite smile. "Congratulations," she said. "You did a great job, and everyone recognized all your hard work, like I knew they would. You were brilliant, Kenan."

"Thank you. But you helped sell it. If not for you on board, the proposal might not have been approved. You had my back—you've always had my back. Eve," he murmured, an urgency entering his voice, his hold tightening on her hand. "Give me five minutes. I don't deserve it, but I'm asking for it, anyway. Please."

It was the "please" that did it for her. Not that he'd never said that word to her before, but it wasn't often. And for him to use it now… Well, she didn't have the armor to resist it.

"Fine. Five minutes. I have to get back to work." Not true. She'd taken the day off when Cain called and asked her to come by the office, but Kenan didn't know that. And besides, she did have something work-related to do—write a resignation letter.

"Thanks, sweetheart."

Still grasping her hand, he led her out of the conference room and down the hall to his office. She should remove her hand. Should insist he not touch her. Should do a lot of things. But, dammit, she couldn't. She *wanted* his touch. Missed it.

As soon as they entered his office, she summoned up the strength to withdraw from him. Rubbing her thumb into her palm, she tried to erase the brand of his hand on hers. The craving it stirred for more.

"Thank you, Eve," he murmured, and she tried not to get lost in his blue-gray eyes. "Thank you for coming here, first of all. I didn't think you'd come if I invited you, so I apologize for the subterfuge of putting Cain and Achilles up to it. But I wanted you there for the presentation. First, so you could see the excitement for Intimate Curves and your designs for yourself. Second, for more selfish reasons, I needed you there. I'm at my best with you, and I couldn't have done any of this without you. I didn't expect you to reveal yourself as the owner, but damn, Eve, I've never been so proud. So happy for you."

"I'm proud of myself."

A smile flirted with his mouth and, unlike Nico Morgan, Kenan's pleasure reached his eyes.

"You should be." He held out his hands, studied the palms, then lowered them. And when he lifted his head, she stifled a gasp at the pain in his eyes. "Eve, I don't have the words to express how much I hate that I hurt you. That *I* was the one who caused you pain, who rejected you. Since we were children in that break room, it's been my job to be your soft place to land just as you've been mine. And I tore that safety net out from under you, and I will never forgive myself for that. But I'm not above asking for *your* forgiveness."

He clenched his jaw, the muscle there working.

"Kenan," she whispered, unsure what to say, but he shook his head, cutting her off.

"I haven't been honest with you, Eve. You know I've been searching for information on my birth mother." He paused, and she nodded, frowning. What did that have to do with them? "I recently found out her identity. She's my mother."

"What? I don't... What?"

He nodded. "My adoptive mother is actually my birth mother. She had an affair with Barron Farrell all those years ago and got pregnant. To avoid anyone finding out, my parents decided to pretend I was adopted. And they've lied to me all these years."

"Jesus, Kenan." She went to him, grabbing his hands, clasping them between hers. "I can't... When did you find this out?"

"Last Monday."

I'm through blindly accepting lies just because someone tells me their truths. I'm done being someone's secret and their Plan B. Never again.

Oh, God. She hadn't known what he'd meant by those words at the time. But now she did. He'd just discovered his parents had lied to him for thirty years and then walked up on her and Gavin, thinking she'd betrayed him. No wonder he'd been so hurt and acted so coldly. The knowledge didn't lessen the pain, but she did understand.

"Kenan, I'm sorry. I can't imagine. Are you okay?"

"Yes." He flipped their hands so he held hers in his. "I've talked to my mother, and she and Dad are going to tell Gavin the truth, but there's no point in letting it go past the family. It's going to take some time, but…" He shrugged a shoulder. "I love her, even if I don't know what the future holds. What I do know is I can't see one without you." He stroked his hands up her arms, over her shoulders and neck until he cradled her jaw. "I have another confession. I love you. I've been in love with you for fifteen years. There's never been anyone else who has owned my heart. And when you accused me of being scared, you had no idea how right you were. I've been terrified for half my life of telling you how much I love you. Afraid you could never see me as more than a friend. Afraid of losing you. Afraid I would always be second to Gavin. Rather than take a risk and tell you the truth, I hid the truth. But I'm tired of hiding. I want to live free. With you."

He pressed his forehead to hers, his breath mingling with the soft pants that broke on her lips. Joy, hope and disbelief warred for dominance inside her. He'd been in love with her for years. *Years.* Damn, he was a fantastic actor, because she'd never guessed, never known. So much wasted time. She wanted to kiss the life out of him and smack him in the back of the head.

"Please, sweetheart, don't take your heart from me. Just when I finally had your love, I threw it back at you, and I'm begging you for another chance. You can trust me. I'll spend the rest of my life showing you, proving you can trust me with the most precious thing in this world—your heart."

"No more secrets," she said, circling his wrists. "Complete honesty between us from now on. And I'll start right here…" She tipped back her head farther, met his bright, piercing gaze and basked in the love there as if it was the sun, warming her. "My heart and my trust are yours and only yours. First as my friend and now as the love of my life. I love you, Kenan Rhodes."

Murmuring her name, he bowed his head and kissed her, taking her mouth in a hungry, furious kiss that weakened her knees and sent love and lust spiraling through her.

This man. He did it for her.

And she was claiming him as hers.

Forever.

* * * * *

Can't get enough of
USA TODAY *bestselling author Naima Simone?*

Check out the Blackout Billionaires trilogy.

The Billionaire's Bargain
Black Tie Billionaire
Blame It on the Billionaire

COMING NEXT MONTH FROM

⊕ HARLEQUIN
DESIRE

#2851 RANCHER'S FORGOTTEN RIVAL

The Carsons of Lone Rock • by Maisey Yates

No one infuriates Juniper Sohappy more than ranch owner
Chance Carson. But when Juniper finds him injured and with amnesia
on her property, she must help. He believes he's her ranch hand, and
unexpected passion flares. But when the truth comes to light, will
everything fall apart?

#2852 FROM FEUDING TO FALLING

Texas Cattleman's Club: Fathers and Sons • by Jules Bennett

When Carson Wentworth wins the TCC presidency, tensions flare
between him and rival Lana Langley. But to end their familiy feud and
secure a fortune for the club, Carson needs her—as his fake fiancée. If
they can only ignore the heat between them...

#2853 A SONG OF SECRETS

Hana Trio • by Jayci Lee

After their breakup a decade ago, cellist Angie Han needs composer
Jonathan Shin's song to save her family's organization. Striking
an uneasy truce, they find their attraction still sizzles. But as their
connection grows, will past secrets ruin everything?

#2854 MIDNIGHT SON

Gambling Men • by Barbara Dunlop

Determined to protect his mentor, ruggedly handsome Alaskan
businessman Nathaniel Stone is suspicious of the woman claiming to
be his boss's long-lost daughter, Sophie Crush. He agrees to get close
to her to uncover her intentions, but he cannot ignore their undeniable
attraction...

#2855 MILLION-DOLLAR MIX-UP

The Dunn Brothers • by Jessica Lemmon

With her only client MIA, talent agent Kendall Squire travels to his twin's
luxe mountain cabin to ask him to fill in. But Max Dunn left Hollywood
behind. Now, as they're trapped by a blizzard, things unexpectedly heat
up. Has Kendall found her leading man?

#2856 THE PROBLEM WITH PLAYBOYS

Little Black Book of Secrets • by Karen Booth

Publicist Chloe Burnett is a fixer, and sports agent Parker Sullivan
needs her to take down a vicious gossip account. She never mixes
business with pleasure, but the playboy's hard to resist. When they find
themselves in the account's crosshairs, can their relationship survive?

YOU CAN FIND MORE INFORMATION ON UPCOMING HARLEQUIN TITLES,
FREE EXCERPTS AND MORE AT HARLEQUIN.COM.

HDCNM0122A

SPECIAL EXCERPT FROM

⬢ HARLEQUIN

DESIRE

*Eve Martin has one goal—find her nephew's father—
and her unlikely ally is hotelier Rafael Wentworth, who's
just returned to Texas and the family who abandoned
him. Soon, she's falling hard for the playboy despite
their differences...and their secrets.*

Read on for a sneak peek at
The Rebel's Return, *by Nadine Gonzalez.*

"I'm opening a guesthouse in town, similar to this, but better."

"You're here to check out the competition, aren't you?"

Rafael raised a finger to his lips. "Shh."

"That's sneaky," Eve said with a little smile. "I knew you had a motive for coming here."

He winked. "Just not the motive you thought."

She responded with a roll of the eyes. He noticed her long lashes fanned the high slopes of her cheeks. In the intimate light of the inn's lobby, her skin was smoother than he could have ever imagined.

Rafael was glad the tension that had built up in the car was subsiding. He wanted to make her laugh again, the way she'd laughed when they were alone in the garden. Her laughter had leaped out as if springing from a sealed cave. He'd wanted to take her in his arms and hold her close until she settled down.

"Incoming!"

Lost in the fantasy of holding her, he didn't quite understand what she was saying. "What's that?"

"Just...shut up."

She stepped up to him and brushed her lips to his in a whisper of a kiss. Rafael tensed, the muscles of his abdomen tightening. "Act like you're into it," she murmured through clenched teeth. With every nerve ending in his body setting off sparks, he didn't have to rely on dormant acting skills. He gripped her waist, pulled her close and kissed her hard, deep and slow. She gripped the lapel of his suit jacket and opened to his kiss. He heard her groan just before she tore herself away.

"I think we're good," she said, her voice shaky.

He was shaken, too. "How the hell do you figure?"

"I kissed you to create a distraction," she said. "P&J just walked in."

Paul and Jennifer Carlton were the most annoying couple in Texas, but at this moment he was making plans to send them a fruit basket and a bottle of wine.

"Here I thought you wanted to test that 'sex in an inn' theory."

"Stop thinking that," she scolded. "They're right over there. Don't look now, though."

He wouldn't dream of it. Her swollen lips had his undivided attention.

"Okay… They've entered the dining hall. You can look now."

"Nah. I'll take your word for it."

The manager returned with the keys to their suite, the one with the two distinct and separate bedrooms. The man was a little red in the face from what he'd undoubtedly witnessed.

Rafael plucked the key cards from his hand. "I'll take those. Thanks."

"Anything else, sir?"

"Send up laundry services, will you?" Rafael said. "And your best bottle of tequila."

The manager cleared his throat. "Certainly, sir. Enjoy your evening."

Don't miss what happens next in
The Rebel's Return *by Nadine Gonzalez,*
the next book in the Texas Cattleman's Club:
Fathers and Sons series!

Available February 2022 wherever
Harlequin Desire books and ebooks are sold.

Harlequin.com

HDEXP0122A

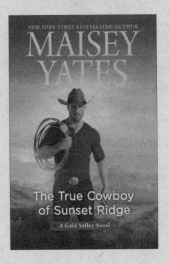

"It's you, isn't it?"

She turned, and there he was.

So close.

Impossibly close.

And she didn't know if she could survive it.

Because those electric blue eyes were looking right into hers. But this time, it wasn't from across a crowded bar. It was right there.

Right there.

And she didn't have a deadweight clinging to her side that kept her from going where she wanted to go, doing what she wanted to do. She was free. Unencumbered, for the first time in fifteen years. For the first damn time.

She was standing there, and she was just Mallory.

Jared wasn't there. Griffin wasn't there. Her parents weren't there.

She was standing on her own, standing there with no one and nothing to tell her what to do, no one and nothing to make her feel a certain thing.

So it was all just him. Blinding electric blue, brilliant and scalding. Perfect.

"I...I think so. Unless...unless you think I'm someone else." It was much less confident and witty than she'd intended. But she didn't feel capable of witty just now.

"You were here once. About six months ago."

He remembered her. He remembered her. This man who had haunted her dreams—no, not haunted, created them—who had filled her mind with erotic imagery that had never existed there before, was…talking about her. He was.

He thought of her. He remembered her.

"I was," she said.

He looked behind her, then back at her. "Where's the boyfriend?"

He asked the question with an edge of hostility. It made her shiver.

"Not here."

"Good." His lips tipped upward into a smile.

"I…" She didn't know what to say. She didn't know what to say because this shimmering feeling inside her was clearly, clearly shared and…

Suddenly her freedom felt terrifying. That freedom that had felt, only a moment before, exhilarating suddenly felt like too much. She wanted to hide. Wanted to scamper under the bar and get behind the bar stool so that she could put something between herself and this electric man. She wondered if she was ready for this.

Because there was no question what this was.

One night.

With nothing at all between them. Nothing but unfamiliar motel bedsheets. A bed she'd never sleep in again and a man she would never sleep with again.

She understood that.

Find out what happens after Mallory and Colt's electrifying night together in
The True Cowboy of Sunset Ridge, *the unmissable final book in Maisey Yates's beloved Gold Valley miniseries!*

Don't miss The True Cowboy of Sunset Ridge *by New York Times bestselling author Maisey Yates, available December 2021 wherever HQN books and ebooks are sold!*

HQNBooks.com